HAUNTED
DARTMOOR

HAUNTED
DARTMOOR

Kevin Hynes

The
History
Press

For Mum

In loving memory of Vivienne Barbara Hynes –
in my thoughts every day.
January 1952 – March 2013

First published 2014

The History Press
The Mill, Brimscombe Port
Stroud, Gloucestershire, GL5 2QG
www.thehistorypress.co.uk

ISBN 978 0 7524 6338 4

Typesetting and origination by The History Press
Printed in Great Britain

CONTENTS

Shaugh Bridge.

ABOUT
THE AUTHOR

KEVIN Hynes was born and brought up in Plymouth. His interest in ghosts and the supernatural stretches back to his early childhood. Over the past ten years Kevin has been actively investigating the paranormal, which includes spending time at a wide array of haunted locations throughout the UK. Previously he has been involved with several paranormal groups, contributing to the running of charity nights and ghost walks, and has appeared on local television and radio in relation to his work.

He co-founded Supernatural Investigations (UK) in 2007 with the aim of conducting in-depth paranormal research. Kevin also founded Haunted Plymouth, which specialises in Plymouth ghost walks, and is the author of *Haunted Plymouth*, also published by The History Press.

www.supernaturalinvestigations.org.uk
www.hauntedplymouth.com

'The oldest and strongest emotion of mankind is fear, and the oldest and strongest kind of fear is fear of the unknown.'

H.P. Lovecraft, 'Supernatural Horror in Literature'

FOREWORD

THERE are few areas of open countryside left in England that can still truly be called wild; one of course is the awe-inspiring stretch of moorland that gets its name from the long-feared river running through it:

'River Dart, River of Dart,
every year thou claimest a heart.'

Dartmoor has both a wealth of historical myths and a very real and modern reputation for the perils travellers risk crossing its open moors and craggy tors. Although much of the moor has been tamed and cultivated, forested areas and treacherous mires also dot the landscape, reminiscent of the legends which occupy almost every boulder across Dartmoor's splendid vista.

Tranquil and serene by day, the site of hundreds of family picnics in the summer, the moor takes on a darker side when night descends or the weather changes, easily disorientating the most hardy walker whilst only a few hundred metres from the sanctuary of their cars.

Small wonder then that to this day tales of pixies still abound – the little people believed to practice their mischief and cause weary feet and tired minds to become 'piskie lead', directing the foolish and lost over the edge of a tor or to a sticky demise in a bog.

This book chronicles some of the many organised investigations into the supernatural on Dartmoor. Many of the accounts given I have had the pleasure and privilege of joining Kevin on, so to summarise and introduce the book in a few hundred words is almost as great a challenge as it would be for one person to cover the entire moor by foot, something not to be advised for safety reasons as much of Dartmoor is so wild and desolate it is used by the army for training purposes, including shooting ranges.

Over the course of fifteen years of investigating the unknown, there have only been a dozen or so occasions when I have either experienced or been with investigators I fully trust who have reported something which might just be genuinely paranormal. Of these experiences, only a handful has involved more than one person reporting exactly the same thing at the same time. The majority of these encounters have been whilst exploring Dartmoor, two in particular were prior to, and indeed the cause of my renewed interest in the paranormal. I won't name the sites as Kevin will detail them within the chapters of this book. If you have had your own encounter perhaps you would like to get in contact with our team, Supernatural Investigations, to share your account. If it turns out to be in the same location, this may make your experience even more unnerving!

One fine sunny day, despite the snowfall during the previous night, my wife-to-be took me to an old quarry, a spot so beautiful that she had suggested it would make a perfect wedding venue. A notion we both soon negated! As we descended into the quarry – and despite the weather not changing at all – we were both overcome with a feeling of dread. This seemed to build and build, to the point where we were both unnerved enough that an alternative venue for lunch had to be sought out. I remember being determined to ascertain what or who might be causing these feelings which had spooked both an experienced hill walker familiar with the area and an adventurous mountain biker, both used to long periods alone in the wild. Perhaps it was the towering quarry walls, leading to a sensation of being surrounded, or the fact that we had earlier come across a pony with its throat torn open, creating a sense that something sinister was watching and waiting. Could we have even disturbed some of the subterranean spirits or

pixies said to dwell in the dark recesses of Dartmoor's old abandoned mine workings? Neither of us are prone to flights of fancy and are both confirmed sceptics, but in my father-in-law's words on hearing our account: 'Something bad happened there …'

On two occasions I have been lucky enough to hear what may be the source of the legends of the little people, once alone and the other whilst in company. The first time was whilst camping on the moor and enjoying a brief spell alone before returning to the shelter of our tents; I heard what I can only loosely describe as a weird bell sound with a metallic, almost synthesised element to it, drifting towards me across the open and brightly moonlit moorland. It truly spooked me. The second occasion, I and others heard an unidentified sound travel across a bank and over a narrow road before fading out after less than a minute, as if a cat with a collar and bell was leaping across the road just a few metres in front of us. Again the weather was fair and visibility excellent, courtesy of the illuminating moonlight.

To reassure the reader, I don't believe in such fabled creatures as fairies, but I am fascinated as to the origins of these tall tales and perplexed at how they have become so enshrined within the popular culture of areas such as Dartmoor and across Cornwall. Equally I cannot offer a rational reason for what I heard, and truly hope that I will enjoy the good fortune to encounter these spectral sounds for a third time, although I do not expect my luck to stretch to being able to fully explain them.

On a more recent trip to the edges of the moor, a feeling of fear descended upon three experienced and not easily scared investigators: all three of us could not stand to be in an area familiar to us, due to our instinct that something most unpleasant would occur if we braved our vigil for much longer. On this occasion the atmosphere was very damp, as it was on perhaps the most compelling experience I have ever had. Well known to our colleagues, who join us from time to time, there was one night in particular when Kevin and I both saw the same thing at the same time ... I shall leave it to my friend to detail the experience within this book as I still struggle to this day to make sense of the events which unfolded.

If you find inspiration within these pages to explore even just a small area of the moor, then do follow the advice offered by the Dartmoor National Park Service: always ensure that someone knows where you are heading and when to expect you back. This is of course in addition to being dressed for all and any weather conditions and having plenty of food and water. Visiting the moor at night or during bad weather should only be undertaken by those with both knowledge of the area and experience. Dartmoor's reputation for dramatically changing weather is not without justification. The weather can literally change within a few minutes and on occasion I have personally witnessed the deterioration from clear visibility to an almost choking fog. I remember one occasion where a small hike of 20 minutes up Crocken Tor took nearly an hour to retrace downhill to discover the road once more. Sever weather conditions can result in a frightening struggle to free yourself from the steely grip of the wilds.

The snow, which can fall heavily, can literally white everything out in minutes, covering both track and road alike. I remember one time when the snow fell so heavily that it caused the wiper linkage in my wife's old car to fail, resulting in a very eerie and cold drive across the legendary Hairy Hands road (B3212) to search out the welcome beacon of the lights from Princetown. With the snow as all-encompassing as it can fall on Dartmoor, small wonder it has been an ideal setting for a prison since the end of the Napoleonic Wars. Heavy snowfall can make tracing your car as dangerous as the drive back across the ice-covered moor itself.

I remember another time whilst Kevin and I were measuring the humidity in the vicinity of Kitty Jay's Grave, and after 5 minutes we were shocked to see how the level shot up to what one can expect to record in a steam room. It was only when we looked up that we realised that a calm and still night had changed and we were literally enveloped in a shroud of mist – fortunately we were less than 10m from

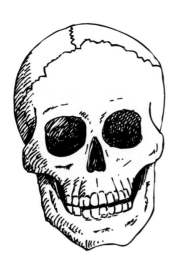

our cars, which was just as well as they had all but disappeared, swallowed up by the night.

So sit back and enjoy this 'tor' of the dark moor and remember, if you pluck up the courage to seek out some of Dartmoor's mysteries for yourself, don't go alone, explore your hunting ground in daylight and never trespass – in summary, stick to the roads and the best of luck!

Stuart Andrews

Co-founder, Supernatural Investigations (UK)
www.si-uk.org.uk
National Register of Professional
Investigators Officer, ASSAP (Association
for the Scientific Study of Anomalous
Phenomena) www.assap.ac.uk

INTRODUCTION & ACKNOWLEDGEMENTS

DARTMOOR is a truly magical landscape with wooded valleys and high granite tors that can be seen by the naked eye for miles. With humans having inhabited this enchanting land as far back as the Bronze Age and beyond, it is no surprise that mankind has left a long-lasting imprint upon the ancient moor. Dartmoor is steeped in folklore and heart-stopping tales of tormented souls wandering aimlessly amongst the abandoned castle ruins and grey granite tors, not to mention the classic local Dartmoor alehouse that has far more spirits to offer – and you know I am not referring to the ones behind the bar!

I have thoroughly enjoyed my time researching and writing *Haunted Dartmoor*. I have had the pleasure of meeting a wide array of local characters along the way, who have been forthcoming with their own personal ghostly encounters. I have also included within the book some of my own paranormal experiences witnessed first-hand over the years that I have spent visiting various haunted locations and sites upon this ancient moorland.

I do hope you enjoy reading the following spine-chilling encounters that I have included within the pages of *Haunted Dartmoor*.

I would like to give my special thanks and gratitude to the following people for their assistance and help in contributing with compiling this book. My appreciation and special thanks must go to my colleagues in Supernatural Investigations (UK) Stuart and Becky Andrews, Clare Buckland and Jason Higgs for all their contributions, time and effort, not to mention the countless paranormal investigations we have undertaken together as an active investigation group. It has been an inspirational and enjoyable journey.

Many thanks to Byron Jackson, the founder of Haunted Devon (www.haunted-devon.co.uk), also fellow author and fantastic writer Laura Quigley. Big thanks to fellow paranormal investigators Beverley Parkes and Sue Powell from Soul Searchers Kernow and many others who have given their time and shared stories of ghostly encounters upon Dartmoor.

Above all else and most importantly I would like to dedicate this book to my wife Gina and my two fantastic children, Sean and Chloe, for their patience and understanding with regards to my passion for the paranormal, and also my father Des Hynes, sister Jenny Allen and especially to all my family and friends – you know who you are.

All photographs in this book, unless otherwise stated, are copyright of the author. I have made every effort to contact copyright holders and gain permission for the use of any copyright material. I apologise if I have inadvertently missed anyone out.

Kevin Hynes, 2014

A-Z OF HAUNTED DARTMOOR

Bearslake Inn

Located along the road from Tavistock to Okehampton is the Bearslake Inn, a sixteenth-century building which is today a popular pub and restaurant. The inn is said to be the haunt of a young girl named Kathy who has been heard weeping and moaning in room number 2 by numerous witnesses over the years. A medium visited the inn a few years ago and picked up on the solemn spirit, stating that Kathy haunts the inn after falling down the staircase to her death.

Berry Pomeroy

Located in a deep wooded gorge, set on the south-east of Dartmoor within 2 miles of the ancient town of Totnes, is the notorious Berry Pomeroy Castle. This ancient castle was originally built in the eleventh century and derived its name from Ralf de la Pomerai, who was bestowed the manor after services rendered during the Battle of Hastings in 1066. A total of nineteen generations of La Pomerais lived at the castle, spanning over 500 years. In 1548 the castle was sold to Edward Seymour, the brother of Jayne Seymour, who became third wife and queen to Henry VIII. The Seymour family invested over £20,000 to construct an impressive luxurious mansion set within the original stone walls of the castle. Five generations of Seymours lived at the castle up until the English Civil War, after which the castle was uninhabited. Left empty, it began to slowly decay for the next 300 years.

Like most castles, Berry Pomeroy has had its fair share of hauntings, with notorious ghosts, spirits and marrow-chilling phantoms witnessed aplenty. To some, Berry Pomeroy is a horror-stricken place where individuals have witnessed first-hand the manifestation of a woman wearing a blue-coloured cape

Berry Pomeroy. (Courtesy of Stuart Andrews)

searching the ancient ruins of the castle for her murdered illegitimate child.

The castle is also said to be the haunt of another female spirit known as the White Lady, who is said to be none other than one of the Pomeroy daughters, who was incarcerated within the cold, dark, dank dungeons of this ancient building. This daughter was allegedly imprisoned by her own sister and left to slowly starve to death. Even during daylight hours some visitors to the castle are only briefly able to visit the dungeon area before hurriedly retreating up the steep stone steps to escape the oppressive feeling of pure dread which is said to fill the air here.

A male apparition has also been sighted within the grounds of the castle over the years; he is described as wearing a tri-corn hat.

I have visited Berry Pomeroy several times during the day and also had the pleasure of spending an evening at this notoriously haunted site in 2006 with Haunted Devon, a local paranormal group. It was a fantastic opportunity to investigate and experience first-hand the alleged paranormal activity at the castle. I have included below my short report summary from that very evening.

Through dowsing I picked up the following information in the Seymour Building:

Kitchen Area

Female 1: Happy to communicate with us; aware she has passed. She passed in 1685, aged 34 years. Cause of death: heart related.

Female 2: This female was also happy to communicate; she had lived in the building when she was alive. Through dowsing I was also able to ascertain her name, which was Isabelle.

Male 1: Once again this presence was happy to communicate and was aware he had passed. He passed in 1785, aged 31. Cause of death: disease. He had worked in the building when he was alive. He was married with two children.

Male 2: This presence was aware he had passed and was also happy to communicate. He passed in 1684, aged 35. He was murdered (stabbed). This male had also worked here when alive.

Elizabethan Great Hall
Through dowsing I picked up on the presence of a man. He had passed in 1414 aged 14. Cause of death was an accident.

Whilst the team moved around the Seymour Building a warm spot was picked up in one particular area. I dowsed to find out what was causing it and picked up on the presence of Isabelle, the female from the kitchen area. The team asked her various questions and we found that she was following us around as she was interested in what we were doing.

I also picked up on a ley line – energy lines that run through the earth – in this area.

The Chapel
In the main chapel area, once again through dowsing, I picked up on the following presences: three males, one female, and negative energy.

The female presence was Isabelle; she was keeping true to her word and following the team around.

One of the male presences was inside the enclosed wooded area of the room. He passed in 1674, cause of death being an accident. During the time I carried out dowsing for this male I had a very tight pain in my chest area, which

I mentioned to the rest of the team. Thankfully this only seemed to last for a short while.

The team did manage to capture a number of anomalies – orbs which appeared as small balls of light – both on still and night vision camera.

Towers
The team also investigated the two towers either side of the main entrance. There was a definite change in atmosphere between the two towers. The tower on the right, as you look at the building from the outside, felt very calming and quiet, whereas the other tower on the left-hand side felt very oppressive and unwelcoming. Myself and another member of the team felt a sensation as if we were being pulled downwards into the ground. Another member seemed to be having trouble keeping her balance, whilst another felt a very warm sensation on her back.

Margaret's Tower
Through dowsing I picked up on two female presences. Once again Isabelle had followed us. The other female presence was named Margaret.

The team carried out a group séance within the tower. Cold spots and breezes were felt by most of the team. Some of the team also felt as if they had been touched. Both Dave and I thought we saw a shadowy movement out of the corner of our eye on the stairs. As we called out for a sign, pretty much on cue the wind seemed to pick up and gust a lot stronger.

Conclusion
A very enjoyable investigation at such a remarkable venue, with some interesting results.

Bradford Pool

This pool is the haunt of a disembodied voice that has been heard calling out to strangers to try and entice them to the water to meet their watery grave.

Brentmoor Manor House

Today all that remains of Brentmoor Manor House is the old stone foundations. You can just make out where certain doorways were once situated when this building was in full use. The house itself is situated upon a level area with the River Avon running just adjacent to the building. At its prime in the eighteenth century, Brentmoor was located in the centre of a 3,000-acre estate, and has had many uses over the years. It was once used as a farm, a holiday home between the First and Second World Wars, and later became a hostel. Unfortunately the house was demolished in 1968 by the new owners, the local water company. I have visited this site on a number of occasions, the first being in November 2012 with my good friend and founder of Haunted Devon, Byron Jackson.

Brentor church. (Courtesy of Desmond Hynes)

It was a cold, moonless night when Byron and I walked along the pathway towards Brentmoor Manor House. There was an eerie silence as we drew closer to the house, the quiet only broken by the sound of the River Avon flowing over the rocky riverbank and the occasional hoot of an owl amongst the trees. As we got closer, the torchlight cast a creepy beam upon the old ruins of Brentmoor Manor House. As I walked amongst the remnants of the old walls I began to feel that we were not alone. I decided to turn to my trusty dowsing rods to see if I could gain any further information. I had 'picked up' two prominent spots and Byron confirmed that both of these areas had been points of interest in the past. I also picked up on a male and female spirit; the male came across as a menacing character and had a strong dislike for women; the female spirit was located by one of the entrance doors and swiftly moved towards the bank leading to the River Avon. I had the impression that the female had some connection with the river. Byron went on to explain that Brentmoor was known to be the haunt of a mournful spirit, a former nanny at the house. It is said that she had smothered an infant before walking down to the river and drowning herself in its icy depths. It is believed that the spirit still re-enacts her sinister crime prior to walking down to the River Avon.

Another lady associated with Brentmoor Manor House is Margaret Meynell, who tragically died in a riding accident in 1865. There is a memorial to her hidden beneath the foliage located to the west of the house.

Brentor

The landmark church of St Michael of the Rock is located upon the ancient volcanic hill of Brentor, 1,100ft above sea level. The first church was constructed around 1130 by Robert Giffard, a wealthy merchant. Legend has it that he built the church after his ship was caught in a treacherous storm off the coast of Devon. At the height of the storm, Giffard called out to St Michael to save him and in return for his life he built a church where he first sighted land. Another folktale has it that the church was attacked by the Devil, who tried his upmost to prevent the building of the church by stealing the foundation stones, but an archangel intervened and threw a gigantic granite rock at the Devil, which struck him between the horns. Brentor itself is located upon the well-known ley line which is said to start at Land's End in West Cornwall and continues through Brentor and on to Glastonbury in Somerset.

Buckland Abbey

Formally a Cistercian monastery which was in a state of ruin prior to being purchased from Sir Richard Grenville by Elizabethan hero Sir Francis Drake in 1581, there are a wide array of curious cases of the supernatural associated with this 700-year-old building.

As well as boasting a fine sixteenth-century Great Hall, the Abbey contains a selection of Drake's paintings and relics, including Drake's Drum, which is said to have accompanied Drake on board his ship the *Golden Hind*. This drum would have beaten out a thunderous call to arms at the onset of battle. The drum is said to have beat out a ghostly tattoo during the First World War in 1915 and once again in 1965, heard by a gardener who stated that he clearly heard the drum beat out. A well-known poem published in 1895 by Sir Henry Newbolt refers to Drake's Drum:

Take my drum to England, hang et by the shore,
Strike et when your powder's runnin' low,
If the Dons sight Devon, I'll quite the port o' Heaven,
An' drum them up the Channel as we drumm'd them long ago.

The spirit of Sir Francis Drake is said to haunt a variety of locations around Devon, including Buckland Abbey, where his ghostly apparition has been witnessed at his former home accompanied by a pack of so-called 'hell hounds'.

There are stories of other ghosts being sighted in and around the Abbey and also rumours of undiscovered tunnels connecting the Abbey to the local village. Legends also abound about Sir Francis Drake being in league with the Devil to ensure the defeat of the Armada.

I have had the fantastic opportunity to investigate Buckland Abbey on

Buckland Abbey. (Courtesy of Desmond Hynes)

two separate occasions. With the kind permission of house manager Jonathan Cummins, I have included my report summary from the last all-night investigation at Buckland Abbey below.

Location: Buckland Abbey, Yelverton,
Devon, PL20 6EY
Date: 5 November 2010
Investigation report summary by Kevin Hynes

The Investigation

The S.I. (UK) team carried out a full investigation to explore the causes of supernatural activity at Buckland Abbey. During the investigation the team gathered information using scientific and psychic methods. We were joined by four members of the National Trust and two volunteers.

The areas that the team investigated were as follows: the chapel, kitchen, the Great Barn, the Great Hall, and the upper-floor area including the Dining Room, museum and Drake's Room.

Roles were discussed upon arrival followed by a brief tour of the location. A time of 30 minutes was allowed for each session, with a 10-minute break before resuming.

20.30 Arrival, followed by introductions and briefing/tour.

22.00 (approx.) Investigation starts.

I split the team into two groups to analyse several main areas, working on a rota exchange system; therefore, each

Buckland Abbey. (Courtesy of Stuart Andrews)

Buckland Abbey. (Courtesy of Stuart Andrews)

group spent approximately 30 minutes in each location. Each investigation team involved the staff present as much as possible. My role for the investigation was Team Overall Leader, Dowsing. I have included a brief summary below of my findings.

Group Séance, the Great Hall

Before we divided into two teams we conducted a group séance in the Great Hall; the reason for this was to invite any sprits' presences to come forward and communicate with the team. It also allowed us to introduce ourselves and state why we were there.

The Chapel

Our first port of call was the chapel. I carried out dowsing in this area and picked up on two male presences that were happy to communicate with us. Overall impressions were that this seemed to be a very peaceful and tranquil area. I had an image in my mind's eye of a woman kneeling at the altar. I felt that she was of great importance to the building and that she had appeared to visitors in the past.

I dowsed for any ley lines in this area and picked a very strong one that runs directly through the location of the altar.

The Kitchen

My first impressions when entering this area were how impressive the kitchen was; it was also drenched in atmosphere and felt very busy. I was drawn to two particular areas, one being to the right of an external door, the other a doorway that led into a small room off the kitchen. I picked up on a male presence by the external doorway. I felt that he was a Scottish gamekeeper and that he was merely warming himself in the kitchen after spending time out in the cold. The other spirit presence I picked up on was a woman by the doorway leading to the small room.

I also dowsed and picked up a ley line that runs through the kitchen.

The Great Barn

This is the most impressive barn I have ever visited; it is enormous and quite overwhelming. I continued to carry out dowsing and picked up on two relevant areas. The first area was by the millstones that were located on the floor and where I picked up on the spirit of a monk once associated with the Abbey; the other area was in the bottom far right-hand side of the barn where a French male presence called Henry indicated he was connected to the land rather than the building.

The Great Hall

The Great Hall was one of my favourite areas purely because of the impressive plasterworks and mouldings – I felt that I could relate to it, being a plasterer by trade! It was a truly fascinating area. In regards to paranormal activity I once again dowsed and picked up on a number of spirits that I was drawn to

Buckland Abbey Chapel. (Courtesy of Stuart Andrews)

Buckland Abbey, the Great Barn. (Courtesy of Stuart Andrews)

beneath my feet and in addition located a number of graves. I also picked up on a man called Richard and was drawn to the door to the left of the fireplace; I felt that this area was very active.

Upper-Floor Area

The upper-floor area was not originally planned to be investigated; Jonathan, the house manager, kindly allowed us to investigate it – as follows:

Dining Room

I spent the majority of my time in the Dining Room area. Here I picked up on a male presence by the window next to the clock. I also felt a female presence, a housemaid from the 1840s.

Museum

The museum area was most impressive, especially with Drake's Drum taking centre stage in the middle of the room. I continued to dowse but did not pick up any presences at the time.

Drake's Room

I spent a very short time in this area but I felt that this area was of great importance and picked up on the active spirit of a male.

Conclusion

I had been looking forward to this investigation for a long time. Buckland Abbey, with its immense history, oozes character and atmosphere and it was an absolute

Buckland Abbey, the Great Hall.

pleasure to investigate such an historic location. I would like to offer my thanks and appreciation to Jonathan Cummins for allowing S.I. (UK) to undertake an all-night investigation at Buckland Abbey and also a big thank you to the National Trust staff and volunteers who joined us.

I personally felt that the investigation was very productive, with some interesting information gathered. The team used a wide array of both scientific (digital and still photography, EMF (electromagnetic field) and EVP (electronic voice phenomena) devices) and psychic methods (pendulum, rod dowsing and psychic mediumship) to communicate with active spirits at Buckland Abbey. The most impressive encounter was when one of our S.I. (UK) members saw a pair of human legs on one of the staircases when none of the team was near the stairs at the time!

Burrator Inn

At Burrator Inn the manifestation of a lady dressed in black has been sighted creeping silently, clutching a bunch of keys. At some point a part of the inn was originally used as a post office and some locals believe the phantom to be the old postmistress.

Cadover Bridge

Legend has it that a spectral manifestation has been seen in the area of Cadover

Bridge. The bloodcurdling sounds of battle and screams of the dying have been heard at this location on Dartmoor. On certain moonlit nights the sound of war horses being ridden hard to battle have also been heard, followed by the sounds of clashing swords and shields.

Castle Inn

The Castle Inn is located in the quaint village of Lydford. Built in 1550, this ancient building oozes atmosphere and character. As soon as you enter the premises you feel that you are stepping back in time: with the lamp-lit bar, old bowed plastered ceilings, slate flagstone floors and an open fire for those crisp winter's nights, this charming local inn sets the scene for a classic haunting.

I have visited the inn on several occasions over the years and have always enjoyed my brief time spent at this impressive location. During one of my last visits I had an interesting conversation with two female members of staff and enquired if either of them had ever encountered anything supernatural at the inn. One of the barmaids said that apparently the phantom of a man is known to haunt the upper-floor rooms and has been sighted on numerous occasions. The barmaid also recalled an incident a number of years previously when they had a number of guests staying at the inn, including a larger-than-life London cabbie who was a bit of a character but nonetheless harmless. On the third morning of the cabbie's stay at the inn, he and the other guests gathered at their usual seats in the restaurant area awaiting their breakfast. It was at this point that the cabbie piped up and asked one of the passing members of staff the whereabouts of the gentleman who had been sitting in the shadowy corner opposite him for the past two mornings at breakfast. The staff member stopped and explained that there had not been any such gentleman sitting in that corner for the past two days. It was at this point that the cabbie turned to the other guests and asked them to confirm that they too had all seen the man yesterday and the day before. To his astonishment all three guests denied knowing who he was talking about. There was a very uncomfortable pause and the cabbie's normally rosy cheeks drained of blood as the staff member suggested that the cabbie must have seen one of the resident ghosts that haunt the Castle Inn. The cabbie slowly stood up, horror-stricken, and explained that he knew what he had seen with his own eyes; he then proceeded to return to his room, pack his bags and check out, unwilling to spend another night at the haunted inn.

The barmaid finally related a particularly unnerving incident involving an Egyptian gentleman who was staying at the Castle for a few days. Upon his arrival at the inn he told the barmaid that he was a psychic and had the ability to see, hear and sense the dead. He told her that the inn was emanating an amazing amount of psychic energy and that the building had the potential to be very active paranormally. The barmaid recommended he should pay a visit to Lydford Castle, situated next to the inn, and also to take a walk down to Lydford Gorge whilst in the area.

Later that afternoon, having taken up the barmaid's suggestion, the gentleman returned looking very much drained and with a stricken look upon his face.

He explained to the barmaid that he had just visited the abandoned ruins of Lydford Castle and described that the castle was a dark, dank, imposing place which was drenched in psychic energy contained within the granite stone of the building. He stated that it was a structure haunted by tormented souls and he felt it was a truly fearsome place to visit, even in daylight hours.

The following day the gentleman decided to visit Lydford Gorge, which is within walking distance of the Castle Inn. Upon his return he was again ashen white with fear and he anxiously told the barmaid what he had experienced at the gorge. He explained that the closer he drew towards Lydford Gorge the more he could feel his heart pounding in his chest. As he walked down towards the gorge he suddenly heard a number of bloodcurdling screams and groans, followed by the imposing feeling of pure doom. The gentleman continued on until he saw a vision that would be etched into his mind for the remainder of his days, for what he saw at the base of the gorge was a hideous replay of human bodies – men, woman and children – who had been incarcerated, tortured and executed at Lydford Castle centuries ago being thrown into the icy black depths of Lydford Gorge. The gentleman said that the whole place needed to be cleansed, exorcised. As I sat at the bar listening to the barmaid recount what the man had encountered, it was very clear that she was genuinely unnerved by retelling the story, and that she would never forget the look in the gentleman's eyes as he told her what he had encountered; it was as if he had come face to face with a number of Lydford's tormented souls.

Chaw Gully Mine

A deep 50ft gash known as Chaw Gully is said to be the haunt of subterranean demons, while others believe the ancient tin mine to be haunted by the Dartmoor Knockers. It is known that the entire area surrounding Chaw Gully is a mass of blocked mine shafts and dark, abandoned tunnels. The mine is known locally to the tinners as Roman Mine; tin was mined here but also gold. Chaw Gully is situated where the boundaries of two tin mines – East Birch Tor Mine and Vitifer Tin Mine – met. Many a hardened tinner stated that Chaw Gully was a doomed, fearsome place and many a tinner lost his life over the centuries trying to extract the precious minerals from beneath the granite-riddled landscape. Legend states that men have been lowered into the blackness on a rope, only to hear the sound of knocking coming from the shadowy bowels of the mine. A sudden glimpse of a claw-like hand grasping a skinny blade is seen looming out of the darkness and attempting to cut the miner's rope so he will plunge to his death. Although today the majority of the mine shafts and tunnels have been filled, it has been said that if you stand in silence and listen, you can hear the evil Dartmoor Knockers trying to entice the next victim into the eerie haunt of Chaw Gully.

Childe's Tomb

Located near Whiteworks is a large granite cross placed upon a heap of granite stones – Childe's Tomb. Childe was a wealthy merchant from the Plymstock area. He was travelling across Dartmoor on horseback in 1340 when he was caught in a treacherous blizzard.

Out of pure desperation he jumped off his horse, killed it and disembowelled it so that he could climb inside to keep warm and out of the freezing elements. Before he died, hidden within his dead horse's carcass and as the blizzard swirled around him, Childe wrote on a small piece of paper the following message:

> The first that brings me to my grave,
> my lands at Plymstock he shall have.

It was the monks from Tavistock Abbey who were to claim Childe's estate in Plymstock. It is said that on wintery days a procession of hooded monks can be seen slowly walking from Childe's Tomb.

Coffin Wood

Coffin Wood is situated within the parish of Lydford on Dartmoor. Eight hundred years ago it was customary to carry the deceased upon tracks and pathways across the moorland to their burial place at Lydford church. The journey over the moorland open to harsh weather could be a dangerous one and it was deemed an easier option to transport the deceased upon a horse, wrapped in a shroud and laid over the horse's back, rather than in a coffin. The sombre journey also incorporated the deceased being taken to the area known as Coffin Wood. Upon arrival the deceased would be transferred to a wooden coffin to be transported the remainder of the journey to their resting place at Lydford.

Within this ancient wooded area apparitions of the ghostly procession of shadow-like figures following a single horse with a shrouded body slung over horseback have been seen.

On dark stormy nights you might perhaps see the flicker of lanterns and hear the sound of mumbling voices within Coffin Wood.

It was also customary during medieval times for the deceased to travel to their resting place via river crossings, as it was believed that spirits could not cross open rivers or streams. It is therefore intriguing to know that Lych Way (lych meaning corpse in Anglo-Saxon) was the route the deceased took. The journey involved crossing a number of major rivers and streams on route to Lydford.

Combestone Tor

This tor is the sombre haunt of Sam Hunnaford, a local Dartmoor farmer. He tragically hanged himself after he had been conned at a local fair. His apparition has been sighted riding his horse and making his last journey home.

Cornwood

Sir Walter Raleigh's widow, Elizabeth Throckmorton, decided to return to her late husband's estate after he was executed at the Tower of London in 1618 on the order of King James.

It is said that Lady Elizabeth returned to Cornwood with her late husband's fortune, for when she died the heirs to the Raleigh estate found evidence that Elizabeth had indeed accumulated a vast amount of wealth, including a large sum of gold coins, yet they were nowhere to be found. Since Lady Elizabeth's death, her spectre has been sighted aimlessly wandering the lanes and fields around the quaint village of Cornwood. She is known by locals as the Dark Lady of Cornwood. She is described as wearing a long black silk dress, and is believed to be instructing those who see her to the whereabouts of the lost Raleigh gold.

Crazywell Pool

Located between Sheepstor and Princetown is the ominous Crazywell Pool, an area steeped in legend and folklore. The pool itself is said to call out the names of the next person to die in the parish of Walkhampton. Thus few local people like to pass within earshot of this black pool of water!

Legend has it that if you were to visit the pool at midnight on midsummer's eve and stare into the water's black abyss the next person to die will be reflected back at you – of course the chances are you are going to see your own reflection! The tale goes that two young men were at a local inn upon the moor when they heard the tale of Crazywell Pool. They laughed at the story but decided to test the legend anyway. Unfortunately, they never had the chance to relate their experience as they were both fatally injured riding their motorcycles home from Crazywell Pool.

Crocken Tor

Located 396m above sea level and said to be the centre of Dartmoor, Crocken Tor was used as a meeting place for the Devonshire Parliament from around the fourteenth to the eighteenth century. Crocken Tor is also home to the menacing Old Crocken, described as 'grey as granite' on a moonlit night,

Crocken Tor. (Courtesy of Stuart Andrews)

Crocken Tor. (Courtesy of Stuart Andrews)

and who is said to ride his spectral horse across the open moor towards Wistman's Wood. Crocken was a huntsman and unites with the spectral Wish Pack hounds every evening at dusk from the ancient tor.

In 2011 I spent a couple of hours on Crocken Tor with my good friend and author Stuart Andrews, quietly waiting to see if Old Crocken would appear. We did not get to see Crocken riding his ghostly steed, however, as a moorland fog came down and enveloped us, and the atmosphere whilst walking back to our cars felt very foreboding.

> '... the gurt old sperit of the moors, old crocken himself, as grey as granite and his eyebrows hanging down over his glimmering eyes like sedge, and his eyes as deep as peat water pools.'
>
> Sabine Baring-Gould (1899)

Dartmoor Inn

Located on the busy Tavistock to Okehampton road is the Dartmoor Inn. This was often a popular stop for travellers heading towards Tavistock and Plymouth. It is said that hauntings at this inn seem to heighten whenever a new landlord takes over. Patrons have witnessed a glass rise up and slowly float down the bar, followed by another glass, before dropping to the floor and shattering into pieces.

Dartmoor Prison

Built by local labour in 1806 and opened in 1809 to house Napoleonic prisoners of war, the prison was later used to house American prisoners of war and the prison population swelled to around 6,000. When prisoners

View towards Dartmoor Prison.

Dartmoor Prison. (Courtesy of Matilda Richards)

passed away they were buried upon the moor. The French and American conflicts came to an end by 1815 and the majority of the prisoners returned to their homelands.

Sightings of deceased inmates have been seen by both prison staff and current inmates in the old burial area and around the prison.

One of the most well-known spirits to haunt Dartmoor Prison is a gentleman named David Davies, imprisoned at Dartmoor from June 1870 to January 1929 after being convicted of over forty theft and burglary offences. He was a model prisoner who enjoyed nothing more than looking after the prison livestock; it is said that he passed away not long after being released, however his ghost returned to the prison and has been seen walking its grounds.

Dewerstone

The Dewerstone, an imposing rocky outcrop which overlooks the River Plym, is steeped in history as it is the site of an Iron Age hill fort. The Celtic name of Dewer means 'Devil'. Legend has it that the Devil himself charges across the haunted realm of Dartmoor each night, heading towards Shaugh Prior and the Dewerstone. The Devil is said to chase lost travellers across the moor, before they fall 150ft to their death from the Devil's Rock at the top of the Dewerstone. Legend states that anyone who catches a glimpse of the Dewer and his pack of Wist Hounds – hellhounds – will be dead within the year.

This area is a well-visited beauty spot with the majority of visitors unaware of the spine-chilling legends associated

The pathway to the Dewerstone.

Shaugh Bridge.

with the darker side of this part of the moor. One well-known legend has it that a local farmer was returning home late one evening from The Warren House Inn when all of a sudden out of the darkness he saw approaching the menacing sight of a hunter accompanied by gigantic hounds with glowing eyes penetrating through the swirling mists. The farmer halted his horse as the huntsman drew closer. Summoning confidence he enquired as to whether the dark-cloaked huntsman had had a good night's hunt, to which the cloaked figure tossed a small bundle towards him. The farmer did not linger and hurried back home to unravel the bundle. Once he had dismounted from his horse he carefully unwrapped the small bundle only to discover the hideous sight of his dead infant child.

Edgcumbe Hotel

In April 2011 I was contacted through a friend by the landlady and landlord of The Edgcumbe Hotel to undertake an all-night investigation into a recent spate of paranormal activity at the inn. Below is a report summary by Jon Small, one of the investigation team.

The Edgcumbe Hotel.

Location: Edgcumbe Hotel, Bere Alston, Devon
Date: 13 May 2011
Investigation report summary by Jon Small

The Edgcumbe Hotel is situated in the village of Bere Alston in Devon. My trip there took me through beautiful lanes filled with bluebells. On arriving in the village my immediate feelings on the hotel were that the night was going to be interesting, and goodness me we weren't disappointed!

We went to the hotel and met the hosts who were very hospitable and the pub itself had a very old-fashioned atmosphere which was lovely. In the pub were regulars who had probably been patrons for years. After our tour and setting up our equipment we decided that it would be boys against girls as we think that separate gender groups get very good results.

The Kitchen

Following a tour of the building, our first area to investigate was the kitchen. Kev, Jason, Chris (on his first investigation), Martin, Dave and I set up our equipment and settled down for our vigil. I was very soon drawn to a spirit lady who introduced herself to me as Florence. She told me that she was 86 when she passed in around 2003. She also told me that she was drawn to one of the men in our group, Chris. At this, Chris went very quiet and seemed to be a bit choked up. Florence seemed a lovely soul and I asked Chris if he may have known this lady and he said he thought she was his late grandmother. Another lady came onto the scene who also appeared to be associated with Chris; she gave Kev the name of Elizabeth and told me that she was a children's nurse but not a resident of the building. Chris confirmed that this was his late great-grandmother. We also had a man come through by the name of Albert who again Chris said that he was associated with. This vigil seemed to be a question and answer time for Chris, even though we were looking for spirits related to the hotel, but as he was a sceptic this was a great start to the evening! The ladies – Florence and Elizabeth – told me that they wanted to protect Chris from a 'male' but there was more to come from this later.

Second-Floor Bedrooms

The second-floor bedrooms consisted of three rooms, including one used for storage and it was here that our hosts told us that they felt uneasy. Another room was now being used by one of our hosts' children. On our tour, three of us had felt uneasy in the child's room and I had felt an uncomfortable tightening across my chest.

We had settled in the child's room and it wasn't long before we heard a few small knocks. I picked up on the spirit of a man who gave me the name

The team during the Edgcumbe investigation.

Edgcumbe Hotel; Jason Higgs setting up equipment

of John. He said that he was something to do with a local mine and gave me the year of 1752. John seemed to be in some sort of managerial position or even an owner as he gave me the impression that he was not of the 'miner type'. We asked lots of questions and John said that he did not mine tin. Martin confirmed that they used to mine arsenic in the mines locally so he was going to investigate this further. John told me that he resented people being in this room as it was the room that he had passed over in and I am fairly sure that this was the spirit that was causing problems through the house. John appeared to be a portly man who had died when he was 61 years of age from a heart attack. The atmosphere in this room was quite cold and John

seemed to be a very troubled soul, but again, more about this later.

The Lounge

The lounge for me was fairly quiet but Martin had the experience of feeling very wobbly here. I was drawn to one area of the lounge – as was one of the others – but I feel that this could have been a vortex area and just highly charged there. Chris was stood in one part of the room and was getting some strange results on his equipment so I went towards him to see what I could pick up. I picked up on the two ladies that we had met earlier in the kitchen and it seemed that they were putting a protective cloak around Chris; again they said that they were protecting him from a male. Albert was in the back-ground again so I thought that this may have been the male, but Chris said there would have been no reason why Albert would have wanted to hurt him. Kevin picked up on another male spirit in the room but apart from that there was no other activity.

The Bar Area and Cellar

This area was very strange as it appeared that one side was active and one side wasn't. We were later told by the hosts that they thought that the building may have once have been two houses which would have explained why all the evidence appeared on one side. We took it in turns to go into the cellar and I went with Kev. The whole area was very flat but Kev thought that the cellar was once much bigger,

which was later confirmed by our hosts. We returned to the bar area and we all felt that there was some sort of movement in or around the bar but nothing was forthcoming. I was attracted to one corner of the bar seating area by a snug and picked up on a spirit gentleman who was sat in his favourite seat. He gave me the name of 'Cleggy' or 'Leggy' and told me that he was 85 when he passed of natural causes in 1982, so we are hoping that someone will be able to identify him. The funny thing was that when Kev asked if he could get him a drink the reply 'Stout' came to me, so that might be a clue for someone.

First-Floor Bedrooms

On the first floor there were two bedrooms and there were reports of

The Edgcumbe bar area.

37

The Edgcumbe bar area.

activity in one room that we weren't aware of. We went to the first room and the area seemed totally flat. There was a high EMF reading coming from one alarm radio, which could have given false feelings of 'something' being there. Our advice to our hosts was that perhaps it was time for a new one! When we went to the second room we picked up a little activity in one corner and three of the group went to the corner and all experienced incredible pains in their back, which was strange, but Dave got the impression that the spirit picked up there was hunched over or may have had a deformity. I was standing at the foot of the bed and picked up on two boys who were there. They gave me the names of Alexander and Richard and the ages of 5 and 9 respectively. They said that they lived in the house but had passed

within a short time of each other from 'The Pox'. The date given was around the 1850s so maybe there are some records of this. The children also said that they were scared of 'the man' and spent their time keeping away from him, so we thought that this might be John who we met upstairs.

Free Time

In our free time, Jason and I decided to go back to the second-floor bedroom as we felt that there was more to get from there. We settled down and it wasn't long before we were in contact with the man known to us as John. We started asking him questions and he seemed very forthcoming. Jason asked if there was a reason why he was trying to scare people in the building and the message we got was that people used to abuse him verbally and he was shunned where he lived. I asked John if he had ever married and his answer was no. Jason asked if there was someone he was in love with but couldn't be with and the answer was yes. I asked if the person he loved was another man and he said yes. Jason asked if he was shunned because people knew of this and there was no answer. I asked if there was a member in our group that reminded him of his love and he said yes. We then ran through the names of our group and when we said the name Chris he said yes, which we deduced was why Chris had so much protection around him this night. We asked why he stayed in the house and he said he was ashamed of what he was and afraid of being judged but he wanted to go. We asked if he wanted our help and he said yes. There were quite a few other knocks in the room and we saw a black shape go from our room to the other bedroom and we thought it may have been the resident cat but when we investigated there was nothing there. Jason and I decided to speak to Kev as we felt that a clearing was needed here to help not only the hosts and their family but to help John too.

We went to the bar area where we met up with our hosts to compare our experiences and we had some very interesting comparisons which was very pleasing. Kev spoke to our hosts about the spirit of John and asked if they would like us to help him over and they agreed that we should. After giving our evidence, Kev, Jason, Clare, Chris and I returned to 'John's' bedroom.

We settled in the room and I again asked for contact with John. It wasn't long before we made contact and again I asked John if he wanted help; he replied yes. I told him that he would not be judged by anyone and he would be able to be with his family again. I asked again if he still wanted our help; his reply was yes. Kev asked him if he could see a bright light, his reply was yes. Kev asked if he could go towards the light; he said yes. Kev asked if he could see anyone in the light that he recognised; he replied yes. Kev asked if it was a member of his family and he said yes. Kev then asked him to reach out and take the hand of that person. He then asked John to go with that person into the light to meet with his family and loved ones. We left it a moment and then Kev dowsed for John but had no reply. I was then asked to do the same and again I had no reply. There were very high emotions in that room and Kev and Chris were visibly moved. The whole area seemed different and the air felt much warmer.

Conclusion

Well, where do I start? The Edgcumbe Hotel was an immense investigation. It was a very draining experience for most of the team but I am glad that we were able to help. I feel that John was a very troubled spirit and only wanted help. Thank you to our hosts for the night and I hope that John has now found peace with his loved ones.

Foggintor Quarry

Location: Foggintor Quarry, Princetown
Date: 25 April 2008
Investigation report summary by
Stuart Andrews

After assembling in the nearby car park at 20.30, the S.I. (UK) team made their way to the quarry, attempting to tour the entire site before darkness descended completely. This investigation was unusual as the site is on open moorland with steep drops and made all the more difficult to navigate by rocks and quarry debris of all shapes and sizes. We therefore kept as one group during this tour, with no formal roles allocated or session times used.

Despite the lack of rain, photography and videoing was made almost impossible due to the high humidity of the night, therefore the photos shown in this report are from a preliminary visit a couple of weeks earlier.

This location had been the site of an unusual experience for myself and Becky, my wife back in 1999:

It had snowed heavily the previous evening, and continued to shower intermittently during the day. There was a mist so typical of a moorland environment for almost the entire day, with it being somewhat overcast. However, this had not dampened our enthusiasm to enjoy the day. I recall as the two of us were walking down through the disused quarry we were singing and joking as two people would normally do, with no thoughts of depression or unsettlement.

Suddenly, as if walking into a field or aura of some sort, my mood changed inexplicably; I began to feel uneasy and aggravated. These feelings came from nowhere, and grew stronger as we neared the bottom of the quarry. Upon reaching the bottom (which is largely covered by a pool of still water) I became more and more uneasy, as if something was watching us. I say 'something' because there were no people visible, and due to us walking around the highest point of the quarry walls no one was visible for miles.

After 5 minutes or so Becky suddenly stated that she wanted to go immediately, and knowing that she is not easily unnerved, and feeling the same, I agreed straightaway. As we were making our way through the quarry, around the pool of water to the opposite side, the feeling of insecurity heightened. Such was the unease felt by Becky that she nearly refused to wait whilst I took a couple of photographs. During the entire time we had been inside the quarry, I had constantly remarked on my feelings, whilst Becky refused to comment. However, once we had left the quarry's vicinity she explained, quite distraught, that she had never ever felt so terrible, or been so glad to leave a place behind her.

Until recently she refused to return there or to even talk about it and became agitated when I questioned her as to what she felt. The reason I mentioned the water and the atmospheric conditions is that the only similar account I have read was that of Thomas Lethbridge at Ladram Bay in Devon when he writes of his theories of magnetic fields with water playing back images and feelings, and the 'ghoul' he experienced. His description of the 'blanket of depression' he felt whilst walking with his wife on the cliffs at Ladram Bay was uncannily similar to our experience at the quarry.

Princetown was named after George IV, when he was Prince Regent. Dartmoor Prison was constructed around 1806 for the housing of French POWs. It was later used to hold American POWs and then used as a factory for the production of naphtha. The local church was

Foggintor Quarry. (Courtesy of Stuart Andrews)

built in 1813 by prisoners from the local jail. The prison was converted to its present use in 1850 to house some of the country's worst criminals. Chain gangs were seen working on the local roads. The quarry below Kings Tor, called Fogging, seems to have been in use for some time and it is likely that the stone could well have been used in the building of the church, which of course would have been constructed before the railway was run round the rather picturesque but torturous route from Yelverton to Princetown.

We began in the area of myself and Becky's experience, now nicknamed 'the steps to Mordor'. Due to the climbing involved most of the team remained at the bottom, opposite the second entrance, nicknamed the 'bog of eternal stench' due to the marshy conditions. Jason and Kev joined Stuart and Becky in making their way up to the top, but were surprised to see how quickly the visibility deterioated, preventing any sight of a view, let alone a serious vigil. After making our way back down, Becky then led the majority of the team back into the central area of the quarry, whilst Stuart remained with Kev and Jenny who were enjoying some results with dowsing. Besides this, there was very little to report from any of the team inside the quarry.

Becky then led one group back towards the ridge and ruined buildings (nicknamed 'Minas Tirith' by Dave, due to its drop into oblivion) via the way we had entered, whilst Stuart led the other half of the team back across the 'bog of eternal stench'. Unfortunately this proved impassable so some more rock climbing was necessary. It was after this and whilst walking back along the disused railway to Minas Tirith that Francesca reported hearing the sound

Fogintor. (Courtesy of Stuart Andrews)

of muffled voices. Though it could have been due to sound reverberating off the quarry walls from the other group, it did not seem to be this and was heard just after Stuart mentioned the convict labour and speculated as to the suffering witnessed by the stones here.

This was the only potentially supernatural experience encountered, although there were some bats which gave me a start! It was a little disappointing that none of the team experienced anything specific, and it was also suprising that the quarry felt peaceful and non-threatening in the dark. Perhaps there is safety in numbers – especially with such a close-knit and experienced team – or was it that we were not there at the right time? Sadly, although not unexpectedly, no conclusions can be drawn, but it was a different and interesting investigation nevertheless.

Gibbet Hill

A truly eerie haunted spot, located high on top of a hill which is not easily visible from the road below. Adeptly named as being the spot where dead bodies were hung and displayed as a warning sign to others who may think twice about not following the law of the land. The corpse would have been placed inside the cold metal gibbet which is a steel type of cage and left to the elements and wild birds to slowly peck and eat away at the deceased rotting corpse.

This area is notorious for the pungent smells of rotting flesh and the sounds of horrific screams of the tormented souls left to sway upon Dartmoor. One victim of Gibbet Hill was hung alive inside the gibbet, and it was a number of days before he died of thirst; on various occasions his guttural screams have been heard begging for someone to put him out of his misery.

Gidleigh Bridge

Gidleigh Bridge is said to be the haunt of a woman who tragically drowned in the river. It is also the site where a skirmish took place during the Civil War and the ghostly sound of battle has been heard.

Globe Inn

The Globe Inn in Chagford is said to be the eerie haunt of a young fourteenth-century chambermaid who was believed to have been a witch and suffered the hideous trial of being ducked to seal her fate. She did indeed drown, which meant she was not a witch, although the law stated that if she had survived the dunking she would then have been burnt at the stake. Either way it was a gruesome end for anyone who was tried for being a so-called witch. As you can imagine, the chambermaid was none too pleased with the bleak ending to her life. She has been encountered in one of the Globe Inn's upper-floor rooms, making her presence felt.

Great Fulford Manor

I had the pleasure of undertaking an investigation with my good friends and fellow investigators from Haunted Devon. With their kind permission I have included the report summary from the night spent at this ancient family home.

History

The Fulford family have made Great Fulford at Dunsford their home since about 1190. The present house is a semi-fortified mansion constructed mainly in the early sixteenth century, although there are a number of seventeenth- and eighteenth-century rooms. The manor was given to William de Fulford by Richard the Lionheart in recognition of gallant service in the Crusades. On 8 July 1402, Bishop Stafford granted a license to Henry Fulford and his wife Wilhelmina to have Divine Service performed. In 1417, Henry Fulford was appointed Sheriff of Cornwall. His descendant, Sir John Fulford, Sheriff of Devon, was the builder of the present Great Fulford House, which was bombarded by Parliamentarian forces in the Civil War.

During the Second World War, Fulford Manor was used as a local boys' boarding school when the pupils of Southey Hall School were evacuated after their school was badly damaged after being bombed during an air raid in October 1940. The classrooms were located on the first floor and the dormitories on the second. The headmaster's office – believed to be the original chapel of the house – was located on the ground floor just to the left as you enter Fulford.

Location: Great Fulford Manor, Dunsford, Exeter, EX6 7AJ
Date: 12 November 2011
Investigation report by Byron Jackson, PR and Media – Haunted Devon

It was a dry, clear, cool evening that saw twenty members – split into two teams – revisit (from May 2011) this fabulous building to continue our investigation; being term-time, more of the building was available to us.

Baseline tests showed nothing of particular note; there was a very high EMF reading from the tumble drier in the kitchen, as would be expected, and had also been noted on our previous visit. Elsewhere, readings varied between 0.2mG and 0.6mG as we would expect (a 'normal' range is between 0.0mG and 0.8mG). The temperature within the building ranged from 17 to 19 degrees and the humidity was around 60 per cent throughout.

The previously out-of-bounds bedroom brought some interesting results in the form of sighs, breathing and footsteps noted by multiple witnesses simultaneously. One team also noted that the temperature dropped quite notice-ably during their time in this room. The names Rose and Jason were picked up by sensitive members in this room. Along the corridor near the kitchen, workshop and scullery several members reported seeing lights moving around. Two members also saw a black figure cross the end of the corridor. Interestingly, in the Great Hall two members on different teams were to come up with the names Robert and Robbie. In the

ballroom, a spirit boy named Michael was found who seemed very scared. The Red Room was to reveal an admiral in a red and black smoking jacket, whilst the old dining room was found to be the haunt of a Molly and a Simon. Two members picked up information relating to the seventeenth century, with one noting an Edward Fulford, a captain during the Civil War who passed in 1641/2, whilst the other picked up the date 1633 and the phrase, 'It was a right royal battle'. Other names picked up by sensitive members were Francis Fulford, Elizabeth Fulford, Philippa, Maria and Margaret.

Green Combe

Situated upon the notoriously haunted B3212 road from Moretonhampstead to Postbridge, Green Combe is an unnerving place to visit after sunset. I have spent a few hours at Green Combe after sundown and can honestly say that

The B3212. (Courtesy of Stuart Andrews)

the area is indeed very atmospheric, especially whilst standing in the darkness listening to the cold waters of the East Bovey River passing under the road. This area is said to be the haunted realm of a short human-shaped creature, said to manifest and run alongside travelling vehicles waving its arms in desperation, as if to warn travellers of danger ahead.

Drivers passing this area have reported feeling a sense of foreboding accompanied by a sudden drop in temperature. One lady driving along the B3212 one afternoon said that she felt such an odd sensation that she stopped a few hundred metres up the road and, cold, she put her coat on. It was then that she noticed her dog cowering and whining on the back seat of her car, obviously frightened by something unseen.

Hairy Hands of Dartmoor

The Hairy Hands is a very well-known ghost story associated with the B3212. My mother told me the story of the Hairy Hands when I was a small boy and from that moment on I was completely fascinated with reading about Dartmoor and its ghostly hauntings and phantoms. I bought one of my first books on the subject when I was 7 years old and have been trying to quench my thirst for knowledge of the paranormal ever since. In many ways it has been a journey and I have now come full circle, having visited the site where the infamous Hairy Hands are said to haunt. I now tell the tale of this curious haunting to my own children!

The curious case of the Hairy Hands dates back over a hundred years, as in 1910 drivers, cyclists and travellers reported a wide array of encounters with a pair of large, disembodied hairy hands. There have been numerous accidents on this particular stretch of road and in most incidents the victims have stated that their vehicle suddenly violently swerved and they lost control, ending up very shaken and drawn to a halt on the verge on the opposite side of the road.

A number of fatalities on this spot have been attributed to the notorious Hairy Hands. In June 1921 a doctor called E.H. Helby, who was working for Dartmoor Prison and had travelled on this road countless times, was killed when he lost control of his motorcycle and sidecar, occupied by two young women. The women were thrown clear and survived the incident, but Dr Helby was less fortunate. This was not to be the last incident to occur that summer, as on 26 August a bus driver lost control on the same stretch of road, throwing a number of people off their seats. The incidents captivated the local press and a newspaper reporter was sent to investigate. A number of people believed the tragic events to have been caused by the adverse camber in the road and the local council acted to reduce it.

On 26 August 1921 an army captain reported that a large pair of hairy hands took control of his motorcycle and forced him off the road.

In 1924 a woman camping in her caravan, located at nearby Powder Mills, awoke early one dark morning to see a large hairy hand slowly creeping up the caravan window. The female was petrified to death as she made the sign of the cross and began to pray. At this point the disembodied hand slowly crept down the window before completely vanishing into thin air.

The B3212.

B3212: The Hairy Hands road team investigating the area.

In 1960 a fatal accident occurred on this lonely stretch of the B3212 when a car was found upturned in a ditch next to the supposed site of where the hairy hands had previously appeared. There were no witnesses to this fatality, no faults with the car, and the cause of the accident was never established.

My brother-in-law, who drives for a living and is very sceptical, was driving his family along the B3212 in 2012 when he had a worrying experience. For a brief moment he had absolutely no control of the car and feared that he was going to crash. However, he managed to regain control of the car and later took it to the garage to have it checked; no fault was found.

Highwayman Inn

The Highwayman Inn is located on the main road from Tavistock to Okehampton. There has been an inn on this site since 1282. Today, the inn is a marvel to behold, the exterior made from wood from a church as well as timber and panelling from an old pirate ship. One of the entrances to this fantastic inn is through an old coach cabin doorway. There are Gothic arches and a wide array of decorative wooden beams and panels which all help to make the Highwayman Inn a very intriguing place to visit.

As you can imagine for such an old building, filled with materials from around the region and beyond, it is no surprise that the inn has its fair share of resident ghosts. One of the more well-known spirits to have been sighted by the inn's

The Highwayman Inn. (Courtesy of Stuart Andrews)

The Highwayman Inn. (Courtesy of Stuart Andrews)

owner is that of a cavalier named Samuel. He is believed to be one of the lost souls who fought in the battle at Sourton Cross during the English Civil War. Samuel – described as wearing a large feather in his hat – is not a retiring spirit and has been witnessed walking the building and disappearing through solid walls.

One of the interior doors is from a ship that tragically sank in 1817, taking no fewer than sixteen hands to Davy Jones' locker. A sea captain named Grenville is said to haunt the bar area. A dark imposing male figure once entered the inn one afternoon, causing the entrance bell above the door to ring, before walking into one of the bar areas and completely vanishing into thin air.

Holy Trinity Church

A total of 196 large stone steps will ascend you to the heights of Holy Trinity church, which is perched upon a rocky outcrop with views overlooking Buckfast Abbey. As you enter the church graveyard you cannot help but notice a very large – what locals describe as a penthouse – tomb, which has a roof and rear door access and metal bars. The curious visitor will discover that this is the resting place for the notorious Squire Richard Cabell who lived during the sixteenth century and was local squire to Buckfastleigh. He had a reputation for being an evil man amongst the locals, who believed that he had sold his soul to Satan. This was one rumour that the people of Buckfastleigh took very seriously, and, if you look through the thick metal bars of Squire Cabell's tomb, you will see a thick-set granite slab placed on top of the tomb. Villagers feared Cabell in life and dreaded the thought that his evil spirit may return after death.

Holy Trinity church.

Squire Cabell passed away on 5 July 1677 and from this point on the hauntings began. It was said that grotesque black hellhounds with demon red eyes were seen stalking in a menacing fashion around the squire's tomb. Villagers purported to have witnessed a whole array of dark, hideous, inhuman creatures that appeared to pay homage to the wicked squire.

Local legend has it that if you pass around the squire's tomb seven times and then place your hand through the gap between the wrought-iron bars, Squire Cabell or the Devil himself will appear and snatch your hand. Beware.

In the nineteenth century the church itself was known to be the haunt of bodysnatchers looking for a freshly buried corpse. Early in the same century it was struck by lightning and then on 8 May 1849 it was attacked by arsonists, later being repaired in 1884. The precious stained-glass windows were shattered by bomb blasts during the Second World War. Finally, on 21 July 1997, at around midnight, a fire was started under the church's altar; unfortunately the fire was so intense that the church could not be saved. Many locals believed the fire was started by Satanists, as the area was known to be a hotspot for devil worshippers.

I have spent some time at Holy Trinity church and can say that once it becomes dark the whole area takes on a different vibe. You do have the feeling you are not alone and being watched by unseen forces.

On one occasion, I and three other people spent around 6 hours at the site trying to capture evidence of paranormal activity. Although I never came face to face with large black monstrous dogs, whilst standing by Squire Cabell's tomb I did feel pure dread and wanted to leave the area — could this have been auto-suggestion?

We decided to spend time in one area that was sheltered from the elements and we called out to encourage any active spirits to give us a sign of their presence. On two occasions a trigger object that was placed on a nearby windowsill flew off with force and landed on the ground. This was witnessed by all four of us. We repeated the process around half an hour later, once again asked for a sign, and once again the trigger object flew to the ground.

Further activity was witnessed by the group, with two of the team seeing the dark silhouette of a figure in one of the church doorways. The team immediately checked the area with high-powered torches but with no evidence of anyone or anything being in the close vicinity.

RAF Harrowbeer

In the late summer of 1987, a woman was photographed whilst sitting in a helicopter at RAF Harrowbeer waiting for the pilot to join her. However, when the photo was developed it clearly showed a mysterious figure sitting in the empty pilot's seat.

During July 1944, a horrific wartime incident occurred at RAF Harrowbeer when a plane crash-landed and one of the plane's wings collided with a bus, severing several passengers' heads.

Phantom airmen wearing their full combat uniforms have also been sighted after sunset.

Hound Tor

This impressive tor is one of my favourite spots upon Dartmoor; it is a truly awe-inspiring location which I have climbed on several occasions. Once you reach the top of Hound Tor the land below peels away and you feel that you are on top of a small mountain; the views from this location are a true wonder. Hound Tor was featured in the film of Sir Arthur Conan Doyle's *The Hound of the Baskervilles* and it was here that the escaped convict from Dartmoor Prison concealed himself amongst the huge granite boulders.

When you walk amongst these boulders you get the sense you are not alone and a number of people have stated that they have noticed a change in the atmosphere, as well as the feeling of being watched. I recall being told the story of a schoolteacher who was visiting the area. He headed down Hound Tor towards the remains of a medieval village at the foot of the tor, where a number of witnesses encountered him mumbling in a foreign language which later turned out to be ancient Hebrew. The teacher had no recollection of speaking in this language and, just a few weeks after, he dropped dead.

I visited this ancient medieval village in May 2013 and it is an interesting site. All that remains are the abandoned ruins in the shadow of Hound Tor; it is believed that the entire village population was decimated by the Black Death. Around dusk I and three colleagues noticed a distinct change in atmosphere and a general feeling of dread came over me. We therefore decided to head back to our parked vehicles, keeping a weather eye open for the so-called apparition of a phantom horse-riding cavalier that is said to haunt the nearby road.

Hunters Tor

Two women riding on Dartmoor near to Hunters Tor had a very unnerving experience when they saw in the not-too-far distance at least a dozen men upon horseback followed by more men on foot. You may think that there is nothing unnerving about this, but the men were all dressed in medieval clothing and accompanied by a pack of grey hounds! The women believed the group to be part of a film cast and so when the group disappeared behind a ridge they climbed up to higher ground to catch another glimpse – but the mysterious group had completely vanished.

Hound Tor: full moon rising. (Courtesy of David Young,)

John Stephens

Stephens's Grave is known to be the resting place of John Stephens, who committed suicide following a broken heart. Like many suicide victims of the time, John was buried in unconsecrated ground. Suicides were buried at a cross-roads in unconsecrated ground so that the tormented soul would not know which way to go if they returned from the dead. John's earth-bound spirit has been described as a large skeletal being wearing a shabby dark grey robe.

Kitty Jay's Grave

Situated on the road between Heatree Cross and Hound Tor you will come across one of the most frequently visited sights upon Dartmoor, Kitty Jay's Grave. There are various versions about who Kitty Jay was and why she was buried at the roadside.

The bare bones of the story are that she was an orphan from a workhouse who worked at Manaton Farm. She was seduced by a young farm labourer and became pregnant, and out of shame and desperation she hanged herself in the farmer's barn.

As was the custom for all suicides at the time, Kitty Jay was buried at the crossroads where three parishes meet; Manaton, North Bovey and Widecombe, with a wooden stake driven through her heart. It has been said that by placing her at this spot each parish had no responsibility for the grave. In 1860, a gentleman called James Bryant excavated the grave to ascertain that a young female was

Kitty Jay's Grave.

indeed buried in this lonely place. Bryant unearthed the remains of a female human skull and bones which he placed in a wooden box and reburied in the same spot with the raised mound that you see today. There has been much interest in Kitty Jay's Grave as for many years fresh flowers were mysteriously placed upon the grave on a daily basis. Even after harsh moorland blizzards, fresh flowers have been left with no sign of footprints left in the thick blanket of white snow.

For me, Kitty Jay's Grave is one of the most, if not *the* most haunted site upon Dartmoor. The reason why I make such a bold statement is that it was at this location that I spent many hours one night trying to capture genuine evidence of the paranormal activity associated with the so-called hauntings of Kitty Jay. I can honestly say that I was left awe-stricken at what I had witnessed first-hand at this notoriously haunted site.

I have included my report from that very active night spent at Kitty Jay's Grave:

Location: Kitty Jay's Grave
Date: 18 August 2007
Investigation report summary by Kevin Hynes

On arrival at this location with Stuart, Dave, Georgia and Debbie, I must state that the area felt very calming indeed, with a sense of peace and quiet; little did I know that in the next 2 hours I was going to experience a wide array of unexplainable activity, ranging from the sounds of footsteps to full-blown apparitions.

00.35

Through dowsing I gathered the following information about a female presence located to the left of Kitty Jay's Grave in the middle of the road.

Kitty Jay's Grave. (Courtesy of Stuart Andrews)

- The female's name is Beatrice.
- She passed in 1734 aged 23.
- She died as a result of childbirth.
- She did not pass in this exact area, but elsewhere.
- She comes in visitation, as the area was significant to her when she was alive.
- She was aware of another presence in this same area.
- I asked Beatrice to point the rods in the direction of the other presence; they pointed in the direction of Stuart and Dave, who were by the car.

Further dowsing revealed that this presence was a negative presence. The presence had been summoned by the use of Ouija boards, from people trying to contact Kitty Jay; they had instead summoned this lower entity.

01.20

- Footsteps were heard from the direction of where Beatrice had been 'picked up' originally. I was at the time reading out the story of Kitty Jay's Grave from a book I had brought with me. As I read out the story I was absolutely shocked to see the name *Beatrice Chase* in the text. I stated to the others in the group that I had not read this story for many years and did not remember a Beatrice. Could this be the same Beatrice who I had picked up through dowsing?
- At this point Dave felt something touch the front of his jacket
- We then all heard the sound of metal clinking, coming from an area where no one was standing.

We all gathered around Stuart's car; Stuart sat in the driver's seat with Dave in the passenger seat and Debbie and Georgia in the rear. I was standing next to the driver's door, speaking to Stuart and facing Debbie and Georgia. Suddenly both myself and Stuart saw what I can only describe as a white mass, that seemed about the size of a carrier bag. This moved from Georgia's

Kitty Jay's Grave. (Courtesy of Stuart Andrews)

right then arched over her shoulder and moved down towards her left shoulder. At this moment Debbie and Georgia both jumped and Georgia went to grab the back of her head. She stated that she had felt something behind her. I was impressed that two people witnessed exactly the same occurrence. Dave did not see anything from where he was seated.

01.50

- Whilst standing opposite Dave, Debbie and Georgia, on the other side of the road, next to Kitty Jay's Grave, I can only describe what I saw as a figure appear to the left of Dave, walking quickly away from him to a stone nearby, and then vanish into thin air. The figure was opaque with a slight blue/grey colouration. This lasted approx. 2 seconds. After this sighting I was so taken back that Stuart advised me to move away from the area for a few moments.

- Georgia commented, not long after this occurrence, that she had been seeing streaks of light throughout the night.

- Stuart proceeded to move forward towards the stone where the figure had disappeared. At this point I was standing to his right and everyone else was to my right. Stuart heard footsteps behind and to his left as he stood in front of the stone. He genuinely thought it was me walking behind him; at this point the activity seemed to be increasing.

- Debbie and Georgia told me what they had picked up earlier whilst dowsing in the area. They had picked up that magic had been used and they also commented on people

wearing dark robes. I was quite shocked with this as I too had picked up that magic had been practiced in this area. It was at this stage that we felt there were a large number of presences surrounding us and the atmosphere did not feel very pleasing. We decided to move away from the area, as the weather was turning against us and the safety of the group was imperative.

Conclusion

I must admit that from the time of arriving at Kitty Jay's Grave I genuinely thought it was going to be a quiet place. Little did I know that it was such an active area! It is quite a strong comment to make, but over the time we spent in this area I experienced more than I have done in the previous five years.

After researching Beatrice Chase, I found out that she was a local author who was apparently responsible for laying flowers upon Jay's Grave during her lifetime. Also, I was absolutely amazed to discover that she was buried in Widecombe churchyard in an open coffin wearing a Dominican robe, which as far as I am aware was white in colour. If this is the case could this have been Beatrice trying to make contact on the night, showing herself behind Debbie and Georgia?

I made a return visit to this location about a week later on Friday, 24 August 2007. Unfortunately the activity was not as forthcoming as the previous week. The moonlit sky was clear, with no wind and rain, which was the complete opposite from the previous visit. I will endeavour to revisit this location, as I feel there are still so many unanswered questions.

Finally, I would like to say a big thank you to Dave, Stuart, Georgia and Debbie for carrying out this investigation in a professional and efficient manner.

Leighbeer Tunnel

Leighbeer Tunnel, also known locally as Shaugh Tunnel, was once part of the railway network that linked the town of Plymouth to Tavistock. Work on the railway commenced in August 1856 with Mr Brampton being the engineer until his sudden death the following year. Mr Brampton was replaced by none other than Isambard Kingdom Brunel.

The opening of the South Devon and Tavistock Railway took place on 21 June 1859, its closure on 31 December 1962. Today the old railway line is used as the Plym Valley cycle path. I recall in my younger years cycling through this tunnel with my friends and even then the tunnel gave off an oppressive atmosphere, especially when in the centre. I recall one venture where four of us cycled from Plymbridge to Leighbeer Tunnel and beyond. Only one of us had lights on our pushbike and it was his role to stay ahead to light the way for us. Halfway through the tunnel his lights completely failed! We couldn't get out quick enough. Today, the tunnel has changed somewhat, as the floor has been concreted and there are lights on a timer (which turn on around 9 p.m.) running through the whole tunnel length.

I am aware of several hauntings associated with Leighbeer Tunnel. My father-in-law grew up in Shaugh Prior and he recalled that whilst riding through the tunnel many years ago, prior to the lights being fitted, he was just about halfway through the dark, dank tunnel when all of a sudden, out of the shadows a large dog leaped forward, brushing against his legs and causing him to swerve and brake to a halt. He shouted to the others who were with him, asking if they saw where the dog went, to which they replied, 'What dog?'

Leighbeer Tunnel.

This story inspired me to research further the hauntings of Leighbeer Tunnel. And so, in the name of research, I have spent several all-night vigils at this eerie haunt.

I have discovered, from personal experience at this location and from talking to individuals from other paranormal groups, that the main area for paranormal activity is in the bend of the tunnel. At this particular spot you can indeed notice the atmosphere change; and with the pitch blackness comes a strong sense of foreboding.

A sighting of an aggressive male spirit has been encountered by several individuals over the past twenty years. This spirit, upon manifesting, is accompanied by a large dog. It is believed by several psychics that the agitated male was once a foreman during construction of the railway. He is a very oppressive and menacing spirit who has been known to push people and is not pleasant to women.

Another ghostly manifestation at Leighbeer Tunnel is a man who is said to have fallen from a train and later died from his injuries. The bone-chilling sight of a figure hanging from the tunnel entrance has allegedly been witnessed in the past.

During a recent investigation my good friend and fellow paranormal investigator Jason Higgs captured a fantastic EVP (electronic voice phenomena) within the mouth of the tunnel at the start of a night's investigation. You can clearly hear a young female voice say, 'Oh no, not again,' which, although bizarre, was not all that unexpected as 'audibles' such

Leighbeer Tunnel.

as horrified screams and the unnerving sound of ponderous footsteps echoing through the tunnel are common at this particular site, though on inspection nothing has ever been found.

The platform located prior to the tunnel is also quite active, as a male spirit has been sighted and is said to haunt this area.

Location: Leighbeer Tunnel
Date: Saturday, 5 May 2012
Investigation report summary by Kevin Hynes

Upon arrival at the location around 7.30 p.m. it was still daylight and this gave the team the ideal opportunity to check out and familiarise themselves with the tunnel and the surrounding area.

This was a return visit to this location as a result of a previous visit back in 2011 when a number of Supernatural Investigations' (UK) core team undertook an all-night vigil to investigate the truth behind the so-called hauntings associated with this location and the surrounding area.

During the first investigation we did in fact experience a wide array of what the team deemed to be paranormal activity. This included Jason picking up a fantastic EVP capture at the beginning of the first group session in the tunnel. We were therefore all curious to see if the team could once again capture some valid evidence from this location.

The Investigation
We were a small team, which was good as I felt that this would reduce the overall contamination from having large numbers. Of course this was an outdoor location and so in many ways we could never rule out human and natural interference compared to an indoor, controlled environment. We therefore stripped back on the amount of technical equipment used, although Jason did still incorporate the use of various EVP recording equipment. I ensured that the MEL meter (which measures both temperature and EMF) and the K2 meter (a type of EMF meter) were used throughout the set sessions and any readings of interest were noted, although overall nothing of great significance was indicated during our time spent at the site.

Our first port of call was the old station platform, where Chris, our guest investigator Jon, Jason and I headed. Chris and Jon both picked up various basic information via dowsing and Chris also stated that he picked up on a number of presences psychically, although from a scientific point of view nothing was detected and validated.

The second session was undertaken in the tunnel. During our first break a number of other people turned up including two investigators from the group Hidden Realms. Chris, the lady from Hidden Realms, was very forthcoming and I recall investigating with her at the Reel Cinema in Plymouth back in 2010. As you can appreciate, having a number of other people now on site affected the overall research. After completing this second session Jason and Graham left and I decided that it would make sense to combine the two teams for the remainder of the investigation.

The remainder of the investigation was mainly spent within the tunnel area. For me, the only activity that I found of interest occurred at approximately 11.55 p.m. Clare took a photograph within the tunnel area, and as her camera flashed, Clare, Chris, Jon and I all saw what we agreed to be a shadowy figure just past mid-tunnel. We ruled out human interference as Stuart was at the other end of the tunnel, and so I started walking towards the area where the figure was seen. I met with Stuart halfway and he confirmed that no one had passed him. Was this, then, a genuine eyewitness account of paranormal activity sighted by four individuals?

Upon inspection of the camera screen Clare said that nothing was clear enough, but I am eager to see if this is still the case once it has been uploaded and viewed on a larger screen.

This was the highlight of the investigation, although all the team members did claim to witness a wide array of strange light anomalies in the tunnel. Was it the human eye trying to adjust to the low light conditions, or did strange lights appear in the tunnel, witnessed by more than one individual?

Conclusion

I would very much like to undertake further research at this location and ideally with only one team present. It is a very interesting site to investigate, from the old platform area to the dark, dank atmosphere of the tunnel. I am interested to see what Chris recorded and to compare this to our previous investigation.

Lych Way

A ghostly funeral procession has been seen moving silently along the old Lych Way, locally known as the Way of the Dead. This mournful scene includes seven men, six of whom are carrying the deceased in a coffin, being led by the seventh man as they wander, heads bowed, towards Lydford.

Lydford Castle

The infamous Lydford Castle was a name known to strike fear into the hearts of many a person during the time that the castle was operational. Built in the thirteenth century, this sombre-looking tower was built upon a large mound and was used as a prison in medieval times. Legend has it that acts of torture and other hideous punishments were undertaken behind these dark, thick-set granite stone walls.

I have visited Lydford Castle on countless occasions over the years and can honestly say that this place has an awe-inspiring atmosphere. Once darkness falls it is as if the abandoned ruins transcend into an eerie haunt for lost souls. I have experienced a range of what I believe to be genuine paranormal activities during my many visits to the castle. On one occasion I was accompanied by a number of friends of mine. During the early hours of the morning I and two others both heard what I can only describe as a horrific gut-wrenching groan, as if someone were taking their last breath. To this day I can still recall the sound clearly in my mind.

One of the most active and menacing spirits that haunt Lydford Castle is a medieval jailer, encountered by many people over the years. He is described as a large dark mass appearing in the doorway to a small room on the lower ground floor. He gives off an oppressive feeling and is accompanied by the sound of metal keys jangling.

Lydford Castle. (Courtesy of Desmond Hynes)

Within the castle, the sound of footsteps and shovelling have been reported – even when no one is moving around.

If you visit Lydford during the day it is worth walking over to the old Norman fort located just behind Lydford church. If you think you are brave enough to visit Lydford during the hours of darkness I am confident that you will at the very least experience the sinister atmosphere that emanates from the ancient castle.

Location: Lydford Castle
Date: August 2007
Investigation report by Kevin Hynes

Historical note: In the Middle Ages, Lydford was the centre of a flourishing tin-mining industry and would have been a very busy place to live. The wealth generated by the area's tin mining brought a lot of official activity to Lydford. For example, there was a royal mint in the town. Large-scale smelting of valuable metals such as lead and silver was carried out in the old town of Lydford. Lydford also had a Royal Court which was renowned for handing out harsh punishments to those who dared break the local stannary laws. A well-known ditty states: 'I oft have heard of Lydford Law how in the morn they hang and draw and sit in judgement after.'

Note: It is believed that at least two ghosts in this village owe their sad existence to Lydford Law. The square granite tower is in the centre of the village. It was believed that the castle was used more as a prison than a castle.

Its very walls plunge deep below ground level; the lower areas are believed to be where the dark, dank dungeons once were situated. In this area many terrible acts, punishments and torture would have been carried out.

It has also been told over many years that within these very stone walls, within the lower part of the keep, a dark opaque mass resembling the shape of a man has been seen on a number of occasions. This whole area is known to give off such an oppressive feeling of pure dread and evil. Those unlucky to have witnessed this do not stay around long after their experience.

It is also believed that Judge Jeffery's haunts this very castle in the form of a large black pig. It is, however, questioned whether Judge Jeffery's ever actually visited Lydford.

Another unnerving tale is that Lady Howard is said to haunt this very location and appears in the form of a black dog.

22.00 – 22.45: Norman fort
Temperature: 10°C
EMF: No reading of significance

- Whilst night-vision filming in this area, Jason sensed that a great battle had occurred here historically.
- Dave and Stu were unable to carry out photography here due to poor weather conditions.
- Sarah commented that she felt short of breath at the front of the fort mound. She felt that the tree on the top gave off a very positive feeling. She also had a very strong sense that many bodies were buried in this area.
- At the same time, Dave, in the lower ditch to the fort mound, said the atmosphere was oppressive and he felt uneasy.
- Debbie and Georgia carried out dowsing.

23.00 – 23.45: Castle area
Temperature: 10–11°C
EMF: 0–0.1mg

- Sarah had a strong feeling of vertigo while on the platform area. The others mentioned this too, but the feeling was not constant.

- A very clear metallic sound was heard from the lower depths of the castle. I must note that I had heard this noise from a previous night vigil at this location – unexplained sounds have been heard whilst calling out. There was, at that present moment in time, no rational explanation for the metallic sound.
- A vortex (in dowsing terms a doorway or portal on a ley line/energy line) was detected by a number of the team whilst dowsing. This vortex confirms the presence of another previously picked up within the lower area of the castle.
- Stuart confirmed the direction of an energy line, again previously detected.
- Overall impressions from Debbie, Georgia and Jason were that something terrible had occurred within this building over many years. They especially felt drawn to one of the lower left-hand areas of the castle. They felt that torture and death played a big part in the oppressive feelings and negative atmosphere experienced.

00.00 – 00.45: Church / graveyard
Temperature: 9–11°C
EMF: No reading

There was nothing of interest to note throughout the time spent in this area by the team members. It seemed a very quiet area indeed.

01.15 – 02.00: Castle grounds
Temperature: 9°C
EMF: No reading

- Jason had a mental image of robe-wearing monks; he also stated that one in particular seemed very apprehensive.

- Debbie, Georgia, Jason and I gathered halfway along the lower ditch which was surrounded by trees and high banks. Debbie and Georgia continued to dowse whilst Jason filmed. Jason felt very sharp head pains and had the impression that someone was murdered in this area. He felt that the male victim was hit over the head with an axe and then dragged along the ground here.
- Whilst in this area Jason commented to me that he had just been bitten on the cheek. On inspection it did look as though he had been scratched on his cheek and Sarah took several photos of this for the report.
- Overall, this area gave off some interesting feelings and impressions although I do feel that the actual area may have had a big influence on this.

Free Time 02.30 – 04.00: Castle area

At this point both teams came together within the thick granite walls to see if any of the castle's former residents would make contact with us.

- Whilst conducting a 'calling out' session, a number of the team heard what was described as keys rattling together.
- Also, whilst a number of the team were gathered on the gangway, a coin fell to the floor between Becky and I, raising more questions than it answered. I felt that the coin was thrown with some force. A perimeter check was carried out by myself and Stuart; no one else was present in the direct vicinity.
- At 03.25 sounds were once again heard by the team; this consisted of the sound of movement, such as footsteps, on gravel.

Lydford Castle.

🐾 I felt something touch the back of my arm by the main entrance, even though I was standing in an open area with nothing and nobody close by.

04.15: End of investigation and debrief

Mary Whiddon

In the year 1641, in the quiet hamlet of Chagford, Mary Whiddon was looking forward to her wedding day. There was one, however, who was not looking forward to the day – the jilted lover Mary had cast aside for the man she was now to marry. The day of Mary's wedding arrived. As she stepped from the horse and carriage she truly looked magnificent in her white wedding dress. Mary slowly walked through the church entrance and smiled as she caught sight of her betrothed standing at the church altar. The wedding service went smoothly and as the newlyweds gracefully left the church they were greeted by the happy locals. Suddenly a loud shot was heard. There was utter panic and commotion. Mary stumbled, clutching her bloodstained chest, as her new husband tried to assist her, but it was too late; the blood slowly drained from Mary Whiddon's fragile body.

Mary was believed to have been shot by her jilted lover, his anger turning to murderous hate. What happened to Mary's murderer is unknown, but you might still see Mary Whiddon's ghost standing in the church doorway.

Chagford Square.

Okehampton Castle

I visited Okehampton Castle in 2013 and was inspired by the sight of this long-abandoned castle. I spoke to a member of the English Heritage staff on site and enquired whether she had ever encountered any of the well-known hauntings and phantoms associated with this illustrious ruin. She quite happily shared her knowledge of two instances experienced by two of her colleagues, the first being the sighting of a very large black dog within the castle grounds where upon further inspection no dog was to be found; the other, the manifestation of Lady Mary Howard's ghost seen at sunrise sitting naked next to the riverbank,

brushing her long hair. I am sure to some this may seem a very welcome paranormal experience!

I have included below, with kind permission, an extract written by friend and fellow author Laura Quigley on her own experience at Okehampton Castle and relevant history associated with the infamous ghost of Lady Mary Howard:

Excerpt from 'The Spirits of Okehampton'
by Laura Quigley, published in Dartmoor Online, www.dartmooronline.co.uk, Issue 2, Spring 2011

My first glimpse of Okehampton Castle came as a surprise. I'd taken so many wrong turns that I was startled by the sudden sight of the ragged towers above a high wall, eerie and malevolent against the wintery sun.

I drove past the sign for the car park, cursing that I'd missed the turn. The ivy-covered walls loomed above me, unsettling my stomach as I frantically looked for a place to turn around. I followed the road back around to where I'd started and finally managed to park the car. And once there I was aware of a growing sense of unease.

I slammed the car door shut behind me, the only sound for miles it seemed. I shivered in the damp air and fastened my coat before heading for the castle grounds dominated by the crumbling towers. Rough piles of stones indicated the remains of vast ballrooms, kitchens and stables. The years had not been kind. The upper floors of bedrooms and servants' quarters had perished into dust and rubble. I wasn't sure what was left to find amongst the ruins.

Okehampton Castle. (Courtesy of Desmond Hynes)

I crossed a small bridge that spanned a gentle brook, the River Okement, and entered the edge of the forest surrounding the area. The castle appeared again, now on my right, the walls shining gold in a burst of sunshine. It appeared deserted. I could see the entrance was on the other side so I retraced my steps and found the ticket booth.

And that was where I stopped. Was someone talking to me? I looked around but I seemed to be the only visitor that day. I glanced at the lady in the ticket booth, flicking through a magazine. No one had spoken.

I took a step towards the ticket booth and the lady looked up expectantly at my approach. But there was the voice again. I studied the ruins ahead of me, the grey stones unmoving in the long grass. As the clouds drifted, a shaft of light burst through the remains of an upper-storey window. Everything was still, silent; there was no movement around me or in the castle grounds. But that voice again, was it in my head?

'You do not want to come in here,' the voice said. I glanced at the ticket lady who frowned at me, puzzled by this strange woman frozen near the entrance. 'You do not want to come in here.'

It was as though the voice was emanating from the castle walls. 'You do not want to come in here' – an ominous, threatening voice in my head. My heart raced. I felt sick, really sick. I turned quickly, rushed back to my car and drove away.

Many will have heard the ghost story of Mary Fitz, also known as Mary Howard, who haunts Okehampton. It has been re-told many times over the centuries; how she appears as a white lady at midnight at the gatehouse of her old home in Tavistock and boards a spectral coach made of human bones, the skulls of her four husbands at each corner, with a headless coachman in the driving seat. A skeletal black dog with fiery eyes accompanies her, running alongside the coach, as she rides across the winding roads of Dartmoor, past the ruins of Lydford Gaol and out towards Okehampton. On arrival at Okehampton Castle, she plucks a blade of grass, and then rides back, all the way back to that gatehouse, back and forth every night from midnight till dawn. She makes this journey every night as penance for her sins, they say, until the end of the world, or until she has taken every blade of grass from Okehampton Castle.

Some say they have seen the demonic dog running along the lane beside the castle. Some say they have seen the coach, and beside the lady sits a spectral white figure, faceless, combing Mary's hair. Many have told the tale, including the famous lyricist and historian Baring Sabine-Gould who related a number of eyewitness accounts.

Others like me, fascinated by the ghost story, have tried to investigate the truth behind it in an effort to explain why Mary Fitz/Howard was damned to this perpetual travelling. My own attempt at making the journey ended with my being unable to enter Okehampton Castle at all. To my eternal embarrassment, I ran away, back through the village and home.

Okehampton Castle, towards the keep.

There has been a village in Okehampton, in the very heart of Dartmoor, from the Iron Age, flourishing through the Bronze Age. Wool production and mining were the principle occupations; the forests cleared for grazing sheep, and the land excavated for surface tin and copper, essential for the manufacture of bronze. (It would be centuries before industry took the people deeper into the earth.) The village was called Ocumundtune in the earliest written records, in 980 AD, meaning the town by the River Okement, and became a vital hub in the trade routes throughout the South West. Saxon barons would regularly ride through Ocumundtune to claim their taxes.

The area was so lucrative, in fact, that within months of the arrival of William the Conqueror in 1066, William sent his cousins and brothers-in-law to build a chain of mound forts along the spine of the South West peninsula: Rougement Castle (after defeating the people of Exeter), Okehampton Castle, Launceston, and west on to Restormel. With the tenacity of their Viking ancestors, now versed in Latin scriptures, these Normans, the name a variant on Norsemen, took absolute control of these precious mining regions. The mound forts were not there to defend the country from invasion but for the invaders to subjugate the locals, and they were very effective.

The Norman Sheriff, Baldwin de Brionne, had married into William's family, and in around 1068 established Okehampton as the administrative centre of his Devon lands. For the Castle, he chose a shale spur on a wooded hillside, and built a mound to support a Norman fort. From there, he would ride out into the surrounding villages and collect his taxes, and supervise the steady supply of wool, tin and copper to the ports on the south Devon coast, to be traded with William's native lands in south-west France. Brionne's heirs – a long line of women – would continue to run the family estates, including Hawisia de Ancourt who married Reginald Courtenay in 1173. At that time, the castle was not much more than a simple motte, a square stone fort atop the hill, with a few rooms and a kitchen around it; a functional arrangement. Reginald Courtenay had grander plans for his new estate.

In France, Reginald Courtenay was born into a prominent family, but

Entrance to Okehampton Castle.

he himself had no land. He accompanied Eleanor of Aquitaine to Britain where she became Queen of England by her marriage to the Norman King Henry II. Reginald was favoured with land in what is now Sutton Courtenay, and established a small manor there, but marriage to Hawisia brought greater fortunes in Devon, and he chose Okehampton Castle to be his stately home. Of course, a simple motte was not nearly impressive enough for a man of his new stature, and he set about building a luxurious castle, with high towers, and many bedrooms, and a vast dining hall for entertaining his many friends. For their entertainment, he developed the forests around into a deer park, still known as Okehampton Park. Reginald was renowned for his sumptuous banquets and hunting parties. There would soon be no landowner in Devon to rival the Courtenays and they held Okehampton for 350 years.

Religious divisions would eventually destroy their fortunes. In the 1500s, Reginald's descendent Henry Courtenay was in a very powerful position. Now Earl of Devon and Marquess of Exeter, he was a cousin and boyhood friend to King Henry VIII, and had a legitimate claim to the throne. From Okehampton, he administered the West of England in his own name, and was due to claim vast lands with Henry VIII's plans for the dissolution of the monasteries. Thomas Cromwell, Henry VIII's chief minister, was jealous of the Courtenays' influence on the monarchy, and set about destroying them. The Courtenays were Catholics, and had maintained an alliance with Henry VIII's first wife, Catherine of Aragon, a Spanish Catholic, now humiliated by the divorce. The Courtenays remained steadfast in their loyalty to the King, but Cromwell informed King Henry that disgruntled Catholics in the South West were plotting to put Henry Courtenay on the throne. There was probably some truth in this; the divorce and subsequent split with the Catholic Church were very unpopular.

King Henry's reaction was brutal. He had Henry Courtenay, his wife, their young son, Edward, and their Catholic allies arrested, imprisoned and brought to trial for treason. The King had Okehampton Castle destroyed, with orders for it never to be rebuilt, as a warning to all who might threaten the throne.

The Courtenays' son and heir Edward, just 12 years old, would remain in prison for the next sixteen years, watching first his father dragged from the cell and beheaded in 1538, and then witnessing his mother and her friends going insane in the horrific prison conditions. Edward's mother was released in time but she was forced to leave her son behind, still trapped alone in a decrepit cell.

Edward was eventually released, much to the delight of the daughter of Catherine of Aragon, now Queen Mary. Mary took a fancy to the handsome Edward, and, both Catholics, there was talk of a marriage, but as in all relationships there was a misunderstanding; Edward thought Mary no longer interested, with talk of her marriage to King Philip of Spain, and Edward tried instead to woo the favour of her younger sister, Elizabeth. This was not a good move. Mary in jealous fury had Edward imprisoned again, then exiled to Europe, where, in Padua, they say, he was poisoned in 1566. It was a sad end to the Courtenay line.

Okehampton Park fared better. A century later, the lands were in the hands of the Fitz family. John Fitz, soon to be knighted by King James I, had married Bridget Courtenay, daughter of the powerful Sir William Courtenay of Powderham Castle on the banks of the River Exe. This Courtenay line had survived and prospered over the centuries, almost equal in power to their predecessors. The deer park provided great sport for Sir John and his friends, though their unruly, drunken behaviour dismayed the puritan community of nearby Tavistock, home to the Fitzs' estates. After accidentally killing two men, Sir John committed suicide, and Okehampton Park with its ruins passed into the hands of his daughter, Mary Fitz.

This wealthy heiress was then married off in quick succession. Her first husband mysteriously died in his sleep. Her second died before he was seventeen. The relations of her third husband, including the powerful Earl of Suffolk, were regularly entertained at Okehampton Park, hunting deer, hare and otter, but her third husband then committed suicide.

In 1628, Mary as a wealthy widow was now old enough to choose her fourth husband for herself, but made a terrible choice, bringing the horror of Sir Richard Grenville to Devon. Sir Richard would become the most sadistic and notorious Royalist General of the English Civil War (1642-1646). He brought death and destruction to Devon, and eventually died in exile in 1658. Their son, also called Richard, was executed as a highwayman in 1652. Mary eventually died alone, leaving all her wealth and property to her cousin, the grandson of Sir William Courtenay of Powderham. At last the castle was back in the hands of the Courtenay family, who in 1750 sold it on to the Duke of Bedford, and eventually the ruins were adopted and maintained by English Heritage. There was an outcry in the 1980s as the New Road joining Okehampton village to the A30 ripped its way through Okehampton Park, but still the park and its ghostly ruins prevail.

View from within Okehampton Castle.

Sketch showing direction of ley line running centre towards the chapel. (Courtesy of Desmond Hynes)

Inside Okehampton Castle keep.

Mary Fitz's name would forever be associated with death, and so the legend was born of the ghostly lady in the spirit coach, driving along Dartmoor roads to Okehampton in the dead of night. But the voice I heard did not belong to a lady. It was a man's voice. 'You do not wish to come in here,' he said. Perhaps it was Henry Courtenay, contemplating the ruins of his family's great manor at Okehampton. Perhaps it was his son, Edward, returning home at last to find it all destroyed. They say the castle looks its best by moonlight, and the towers must be haunting indeed, as the pale light glimmers through the ravaged windows, well worth the journey across Dartmoor to discover it, but you would not see me setting foot there again, not for all the Courtenays' fortunes.

Below with permission is given Clare Buckland's brief report summary from her visit to Okehampton Castle in 2006:

Location: Okehampton Castle
Date: 11 August 2006
Investigation report summary by Clare Buckland

Team members: Clare, Dave, John, Clive
Average air temperature: 12°C approx.
Weather conditions: Dry and overcast but warm
Time of arrival: 9.10 p.m.

Ancient doorway at Okehampton Castle. (Courtesy of Desmond Hynes)

Brief History

Okehampton Castle is an impressive stone motte-and-bailey fortress, founded by Baldwin de Brioni in the eleventh century, soon after the Norman Conquest. The two-storey square keep was added in the fourteenth century and converted into a sumptuous residence by Hugh Courtenay, Earl of Devon. After the last Courtenay owner fell foul of Henry VIII in 1538, it declined into an allegedly haunted ruin. In the grounds there are the remains of lodgings, kitchens, a chapel, a hall and a solar. It is the largest castle in Devon and stands against the steep banks of the River Okement.

The Investigation – 9.30 p.m.

We started our investigation in one of the small rooms on the left of the castle. John dowsed in this area and detected one male and one female presence. The female presence is grounded and died in the building. She died in 1735 aged 42 years. Possible name Elizabeth. She was married and her husband is the male presence in the room. Possible name Henry. He was 44 years old when he died in 1722. His family owned the castle.

I got the impression that there was a woman seated in the upstairs window looking out towards town. She seemed to be crying for her lover. Clive felt someone touch him in this room and also got the impression that there was a female presence there.

We moved out into the larger area adjacent to the small room and John picked up on Elizabeth again. A photo was taken in this area as John was dowsing. After the photo was taken John asked Elizabeth if she was trying to show herself and she replied positively.

John also picked up on two vortices in this area joined by a ley line; one that ran anticlockwise and the other in a clockwise motion. Possibly an in and out 'doorway'?

I saw a hazy blue shape on the lawned area between the castle remains. It could have been glare from a torch or from a car headlight, but it did coincide with us communicating with Elizabeth.

The Great Hall – 10.30 p.m.

Three presences were detected in this area of the castle: one standing in the middle of the room, one by the bench and one by the old doorway.

Henry has followed us into this area and is the presence standing near the bench. One male presence was detected by the doorway and is a grounded male. He died in 1832 aged 24 years. Possible name Cedric. He was part of a team who were restoring the castle when he died of pneumonia. He was a labourer. He can see the other presences in the castle and knows there are seven grounded presences, although more come back in visitation.

Clive picked up on a female presence near one of the old windows – he can smell her perfume. Her name was Rose Sweeny and she worked in the kitchen area of the castle. She was 50 years old when she was murdered by a man called Edward. He didn't want her to leave the castle and get married. Clive also detected the presence of his first cousin in the Great Hall. Whilst in the church area he became very distressed because of a female presence. She was stabbed in the church by Edward. Clive felt like he was being pushed to the ground and throttled. Later he had his sleeve tugged on and heard a tapping noise in the same area.

The Keep – 12.10 a.m.

Two male presences were detected by John in this area. The first one died in 1232 aged 32 years. He died of natural causes or an illness and is grounded here. Possible name Dels–. The second male presence passed in 1325 aged 34 years. He died of smallpox. A female presence was discovered in the entrance to the keep. She died in 1196 aged 23 years old.

She was hanged from a tree for stealing bread from a nearby house.

Final Comments

Okehampton Castle is a very imposing medieval fortress that still holds much of its former mysticism. We experienced a quiet night with much of the castle feeling pleasant and safe.

Old Inn, The

Old Harry is the illustrious ghost that haunts this quiet village inn. This active spirit likes to walk amongst the living and apparently is as plain to see as you or I and it is not unusual for people to move aside for him as he strolls through the bar area. Everything seems quite normal until Harry walks straight into a solid wall and disappears without a trace, leaving behind witnesses with their jaws dropping with pure fright.

Phantom Horse Rider

The illustrious apparition of a man with silver hair is said to haunt the road between Haytor and Widecombe at the base of Rippon Tor. The nebulas ghost has been sighted wearing an old military-style jacket and riding his horse, galloping at full speed before vanishing into thin air.

The Old Inn.

Plume of Feathers

The highest town in England, Princetown is host to a number of public houses, one of which is the Plume of Feathers. Built in 1785, it is the oldest building in Princetown. It therefore comes as no surprise that the inn has had its fair share of ghosts, phantoms and hauntings, making their presences felt to the living of today.

The ladies restrooms are said to have caused a bit of a scare for patrons in the past when a disembodied female voice has been heard crying; it is believed this sad spirit is that of a mother weeping over the death of her child.

On other occasions a number of guests staying at the public house claimed that whilst lying in bed they had felt a strong unseen force pulling at the bed sheets.

Phantom footsteps have also been heard and a woman dressed in a brown cloak was reported to have been seen walking the ground floor. On further inspection, the landlord found no sign of anyone fitting the woman's description.

Plymbridge Woods

Plymbridge Woods is a large oak woodland set against the stunning backdrop of the River Plym. The old Great Western Railway track once ran from the outskirts of Plymouth through this enchanting woodland at Plymbridge and further into the countryside. Today the old railway track is used by families and individuals for walking or cycling. Back in the eighteenth century,

Plymbridge Woods was a bustling place to be as frequent trains were used to transport the local workforce to several slate quarries and also transport granite from Dartmoor.

I decided to take a team of paranormal investigators out to Plymbridge Woods to undertake an all-night investigation at a number of so-called paranormally active sites set within this pleasant setting. Below is an investigation report by Clare Buckland with details of our time spent at Plymbridge Woods.

Location: Plymbridge Woods
Date: 15 August 2006
Investigation report summary by Clare Buckland

22.00: Rumple Quarry
Average temp: 13.5°C
EMF: No unusual readings
Photography: A few light anomalies caught but could have been insects or moisture

Through dowsing, I picked up on a female just inside the doorway to the building, and Sarah felt unsteady on her feet at the far end. Kev picked up on a male and female presence. The female was where I had detected her and the male was on the other side of the doorway. The male presence died in 1882 aged 27 years. He didn't work here but had visited it with his family. The female presence was a tea-maid or helper in the building.

Stu felt that this building was used for dressing, weighing and washing the stone before it was loaded onto trains. Jason felt that a child of 8–10 years may have died in an accident on the site. He was crushed in an accident and died some weeks later from his injuries. He had been helping the workers on the site; not sure of a year but he was wearing Victorian clothing.

Outside the building in the quarry itself, Kev picked up on two male spirits who had died as a result of an accident in the quarry; the quarry wall had fallen on them and they had died near the building.

Sarah picked up on a little girl called Elizabeth from the Victorian era; she was wearing a white pinafore.

Sarah saw dim white lights in the trees back towards the bridge where the other team was on their vigil. We radioed them and asked if they were taking photos, but they hadn't been.

23.00: Under the Bridge
Average temp: 14°C
EMF: No unusual readings
Photography: A few light anomalies caught but could have been insects or moisture.
Jason photographed a moving light anomaly

Stuart and Sarah didn't pick anything up with the dowsing rods initially. This area is unusual because it appears to have a floor surrounded by a low brick wall. No one could explain what this area was used for.

Sarah eventually felt that a female presence had entered the area. She was standing near the steps from the low wall. She had died aged 28–30 years. Sarah dowsed that she was in visitation, but Jason felt that she was grounded to the area and walks on the bridge above us. Jason felt that she was connected to the last war, because he could hear air-raid sirens. She was wearing an auxiliary nurse uniform with a large red cross on her apron. Sarah dowsed for a name and got Gemma. She had jumped off the bridge because of unrequited love.

Stuart continued to dowse, trying to find out a purpose for the strange location. He felt that this was a storage area for railway sleepers and then later was used during the last war to store army materials.

00.50: Cann House
Average temp: 15°C
EMF: No unusual readings
Photography: A few light anomalies caught but could have been insects or moisture.
Halfway through the vigil it started to rain so photography was abandoned

Sarah thought she saw a dark shape standing in the middle of the house ruins. Through dowsing, Kev picked up three males and two females. One of the males had died 14 June 1823 aged 29 years; he lived here and was the son of the owner. He died of a chest-related illness. The female is his wife; she died in a fire in 1834, aged 37 years. She is in visitation but her husband is grounded here. His name is Gerald Feegan, his wife is called Beth.

Jason picked up on a little girl who had fallen from a tree just outside the building and a male presence who had a bald head and a handlebar moustache. He was wearing a collarless shirt and he was about 50 years old.

Sarah felt herself being rocked back and forth.

02.30: Railway Cottages
Average temp: 16°C (drizzly rain – heavy at times)
EMF: No unusual readings
Photography: A few light anomalies caught but could have been insects or moisture.
Halfway through the vigil it started to rain so photography was abandoned

Sarah, Clare and Jason felt the end room was very oppressive and we felt as if there was someone watching us from the doorway. Jason had a headache whilst standing in the doorway to the end room. We felt there was something negative in the area of the house. Jason felt that there was a gentleman walking towards him. He was 30 or 40 years old and was wearing a bowler hat, a brown waistcoat and had a moustache. He was working class. Jason felt that there had been an argument between two men in this room. The man in this room used to beat up his wife and she could be seen sobbing in the corner of the room. Sarah dowsed and picked up on energy near the doorway; it was not connected with the house, and it wasn't male or female.

Further along in one of the main rooms, Sarah picked up on a female presence. She was the lover of someone who had lived in the house. They weren't married conventionally because of their religious backgrounds, no one knew they were a couple and they had no children. She was Spanish and he was English. They had Pagan beliefs and weren't considered married in the eyes of the law. Sarah was picking up the year 1858 with this female. She had been the housekeeper for the family at Cann House and wasn't allowed to live in the cottages with her husband.

Overall Comments
A very interesting night was had in Plymbridge Woods. It is certainly an eerie place at night and the information from the dowsers was very specific. It would be very interesting to find out if any of the information could be tracked down in records.

Ring O'Bells

The article below is reproduced with the kind permission of the landlady at the Ring O'Bells:

The Exeter archives reveal that there has been an inn on the site of the Ring O'Bells since well before the sixteenth century, although it was much smaller than it is today and has twice in its history been destroyed by fire.

The upper part of the front of the building was the site of the Stannary Courts – the body of people responsible for the weighing and assaying of tin and silver found on Dartmoor which would, by law, have to receive the King's Stamp before being sold. The royal personage received a tax from the tinners as a result of their endeavours!

The middle upper part of the Ring O'Bells was used as a holding prison for miscreants en route to Okehampton Assizes. They were kept overnight here having been marched on foot over the moor.

At the rear, again on the first floor, was a Crowners Court (known today as a Coroners Court) also a mortuary and the place where post mortems were carried out in the event of any unusual deaths or suicides. Things that go bump in the night are not unusual!

The Ring O'Bells.

The Ring O'Bells.

Should a death have been a result of a suicide then the unfortunate departed could not, at one time, be buried in the churchyard. Custom dictated that the body be taken to a crossroads and buried there in the presence of the local constable.

Today the Ring O'Bells encompasses the whole site although in years past the ground floor was occupied by a butcher and the beasts were slaughtered in the barn which used to stand in the rear courtyard. Not so many years ago the stone barn was demolished and now there is a pretty walled courtyard garden to the rear of the building instead.

(www.ringobellschagford.co.uk/history)

River Dart

As my good friend and fellow paranormal investigator Stuart Andrews stated in the foreword, the old River Dart is a very rapid-flowing river and at times the noise from it can be quite thunderous in certain areas, as it flows and rushes at speed. Some locals believe it is the cry of the River Dart calling for a heart.

One of the River Dart's victims was a young farmhand from Rowbrook, who is said to have been so obsessed with the menacing stories of the river that one night he ventured into the darkness in the direction of the River Dart screaming, 'The Dart's calling me!' He was never seen again.

The George

This fourteenth-century building is said to have its fair share of spectres and none more so than a phantom stagecoach which has been heard pulling to a standstill outside this quaint inn. Behind these thick granite walls, visitors have experienced bone-chilling cold spots in certain areas of the inn with no natural causes to be found.

The shrouded figure of a woman surrounded by a bright light has also been seen by a number of people.

Three Crowns

A cavalier, believed to be none other than Sidney Godolphin, has been seen in the doorway of this very inn. Godolphin was mortally wounded by a musket shot during a brave skirmish during the English Civil War. His ghost has also been seen walking an ancient corridor of the Three Crowns. A customer staying at the inn identified the illustrious ghost by pointing to one of the paintings of Godophin which hung upon the wall in the inn and stating that he had seen the same gentleman in the corridor that night!

The Three Crowns, Chagford.

The Three Crowns.

Throwleigh

Beware in the darkest hours of the night, as the sounds of invisible creatures running apace have been heard. Those unfortunate enough to have experienced this mysterious occurrence have stated that they could hear the creatures and feel the movement of air as they rushed past them.

One dark, dank evening a young woman and her parents had a heart-stopping experience as they walked down Petticoat Lane which leads down from the moor. The sounds of horses' hooves were clearly heard approaching from behind and so they moved aside into a doorway to wait for the party to pass by. To their absolute amazement the clear sound of horses' hooves passed them by, accompanied by the swirl of air created by movement – but nothing was to be seen. The family stood in shock, listening to the sound of horses' hooves as they faded into the night.

Tunhill Kistvaen

Tunhill Kistvaen is a Bronze Age tomb which once contained the remains of a pre-historic warrior. Legend has it that it was here on 21 October 1631 that Jan Reynolds met a tall, dark, cloaked stranger who purchased Jan's soul in return for seven years of good luck and fortune. Thus, seven years later in 1638, the Devil came in person to Widecombe church to collect his debt and in the process took Jan Reynolds and three other souls during the great fire at Widecombe church.

Valiant Solider, The

My good friends and fellow paranormal investigators from Haunted Devon undertook an investigation at the Valiant Solider in May 2011. With kind permission I have included the report from the investigation below:

Location: The Valiant Soldier pub
Date: May 2011
Investigation report summary by Byron Jackson, PR and Media – Haunted Devon

This venue is unique in the fact that parts of the building are still exactly as they were some fifty years ago. It was a working pub until 1965 when the brewery made the decision that there were too many public houses in the town already so withdrew the licence. In 1969, the landlord passed away, leaving his wife to live there alone until 1996. From the time of the landlord's death, his widow lived only in the bar, leaving the living quarters untouched until her own death in 2000.

The venue lends itself perfectly to three teams, having the barn as one zone, upstairs as another and the downstairs bar, lounge and kitchen as a third. Each team rotated through the zones in one-hour stints. The investigation was filmed by Byron.

Due to the weather conditions, investigating the barn proved difficult, although sensitive team members were able to gather some information which proved relevant.

Results
In the barn area, members picked up on a suicide and the presence of two men; this was confirmed during debrief to be a verified fact. Names sensitive members picked up on in this area were Bruce, Dominic, Colin and Lionel. No evidence was collected here.

In the bar, an event was repeated which the team had experienced previously, in that a blind at the window fell down. It was confirmed by staff the blind had been checked prior to HD's arrival and was found to be secure. In the area behind the bar, some members reported being touched throughout the evening. Attempts to encourage contact were unsuccessful. A voice was picked up in the lounge area saying, 'Excuse me' – this was not heard at the time, but is clearly heard on more than one piece of equipment. Interestingly, a member heard the same phrase spoken during a break in the safe room.

Upstairs, there was little in the way of activity. Names picked up in the living accommodation were John or Jack, Deborah and Mary/Maria. One team did report hearing keys jangling in this area. The evening was quieter than expected, but members still found it a very enjoyable venue. A return will be inevitable when it is hoped there will be more activity. Work is planned throughout the building, opening up rooms which have been unused for some time, so it will be exciting to see what difference this makes.

Warren House Inn

Located on the road from Moretonhampstead to Postbridge, this isolated drinking house has been frequently used by locals and weary travellers for the past 200 years. The original inn was situated on the opposite side of the road to where it now stands. Today you can still see the original flagstones and foundations of this ancient inn. It is said that the fire at the Warren House Inn has never been extinguished and has been alight for over 150 years. When the new Warren House Inn was being constructed they transferred the glowing red embers from one side of the road to the other, where it has continued to burn today. It is believed that if the fire is ever extinguished it will be the end of the world as we know it.

As you stand at the isolated spot occupied by the Warren House Inn you can only imagine what a lonely and remote life it must have been for the innkeeper and his family 200 years ago. A weary traveller many years ago was caught in a blizzard and stopped at the Warren House Inn for a warm meal and a bed for the night. The gentleman was shown to his room where he could not help but notice a large wooden chest. He sat wearily on the edge of his bed staring at the chest, contemplating what was contained within it. His curiosity got the better of him and he lifted the ornate wooden lid, only to discover to his horror the corpse of an elderly gentleman whose

Beertor Cross.

face was as white as the Dartmoor snow. The gentleman swiftly retreated downstairs to the bar area, exclaiming over his gruesome discovery. He had thought that he had uncovered a murder victim, but was relieved when told by the landlord that the body was his elderly father, who had passed away a couple of weeks earlier. Due to the poor weather conditions the corpse had been covered in salt to preserve him until the weather passed and his father could be carried across the moor to be buried.

Watching Place, The

The Watching Place, also known as Beetor Cross, is a large cross found in the hedge line situated on the B3212 road. It is said that the area was once the haunt of a highwayman named John Fall, hence the name 'watching place'; he would wait at the cross and watch for his next victim.

Another reason given for the name is that a gibbet once stood nearby on the crossroads, where executed felons would hang as a hideous warning to others contemplating a life of crime.

The Watching Place.

Widecombe-in-the-Moor

On Sunday, 21 October 1639 the church of St Pancras in Widecombe filled with no fewer than 300 people for the regular service – but one which was to be remembered for all eternity …

Unknown to the locals, a violent thunderstorm was heading for the small peaceful village. Suddenly, the sky

The grave of Beatrice Chase in Widecombe graveyard. (Courtesy of Desmond Hynes)

Widecombe-in-the-Moor.

Inside Widecombe church.

Widecombe church.

turned pitch black, the air felt charged and there was a huge flash followed by a gigantic crack of thunder. A huge explosion of sound ripped through the church – a thunderbolt had smashed through the church tower, sending shards of glass and falling debris into the congregation below. Amidst the panic and confusion some members of the congregation were set alight from the burning timbers. Four people were killed. Some locals believed the tragedy to be the work of the Devil himself. One favourite folktale stated that an hour before the tragic event, a visitor entered an inn at Poundsgate and asked the innkeeper for directions to Widecombe. Of course the innkeeper obliged with the information as he passed over the stranger's flagon of ale, but that as the stranger gulped his drink the sound of sizzling came from his throat. It was at this point that the innkeeper is said to have caught sight of the stranger's cloven hoof. Could this have been the Devil himself?

Wistman's Woods

The enchanting Wistman's Wood, near Two Bridges, is one of the highest oak woodlands in Britain and is a Site of Special Scientific Interest. The name Wistman's Wood is said to derive from the word 'Wisht', meaning spooky. The wood is synonymous with being haunted by the demonic Wist Hounds who set off from this wooded lair in their search for lost travellers and unbaptised souls.

AFTERWORD

I do hope you have enjoyed reading about haunted Dartmoor and that I have inspired you to visit the sites mentioned. If you do intend to venture out upon the ancient moor in search of phantoms, ghosts and mysterious haunts, take care and ensure you stay safe.

BIBLIOGRAPHY & FURTHER READING

Books

Andrews, S. and J. Higgs, *Paranormal Cornwall* (The History Press, 2010)

Bamberg, R.W., *Haunted Dartmoor* (Peninsula Press, 1993)

Brown, T., *Devon Ghosts* (Jarrold & Sons Ltd, 1982)

Chard, J., *Haunted Happenings* (Obelisk Publications, 1988)

Endacott, A., *Okehampton Castle* (English Heritage, 2003)

Higgs, J., *Haunted Bodmin Moor* (The History Press, 2012)

Holgate, M., *Celebrity Ghosts of Devon* (Obelisk Publications, 2003)

Jones, R., *Haunted Britain and Ireland* (New Holland Publishers Ltd, 2001)

Karl, J., *Great Ghost Hunt* (New Holland Publishers Ltd, 2004)

Matthews, R., *The Ghosthunter's Guide to England* (Countryside Books, 2006)

Moiser, C., *Mystery Cats of Devon and Cornwall* (Bossiney Books, 2005)

Neal, A., *Dowsing in Devon and Cornwall* (Bossiney Books, 2001)

Neal, A., *Ley Lines of the South West* (Bossiney Books, 2004)

Quigley, L., *The Devil comes to Dartmoor* (The History Press, 2011)

Seymour, D., *The Ghosts of Berry Pomeroy Castle* (Obelisk, 1996)

St Leger-Gordon, R.E., *The Witchcraft and Folklore of Dartmoor* (Peninsula Press, 2001)

Underwood, P., *Ghosts of Devon* (Bossiney Books, 2003)

Underwood, P., *West Country Hauntings* (Bossiney Books, 2004)

Various authors, *Folklore, Myths and Legends* (Readers Digest, 1977)

Westwood & Simpson, *The Penguin Book of Ghosts* (Penguin Books, 2008)

Williams, M., *Supernatural Dartmoor* (Bossiney Books, 2003)

Williams, M., *Ghost Hunting South-West* (Bossiney Books, 2005).

Websites

www.davidwyoung.co.uk
www.dhosthunteratlarge.blogspot.co.uk
www.hha.org.uk
www.haunted-devon.co.uk

www.hauntedplymouth.com
www.legendarydartmoor.co.uk
www.paranormaldatabase.com
www.ringobellschagford.co.uk/history
www.soulsearcherskernow.com
www.supernaturalinvestigations.org.uk

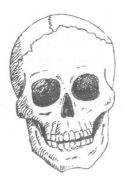

If you enjoyed this book, you may also be interested in …

The Devil Comes to Dartmoor
LAURA QUIGLEY

Many will have heard of the notorious Mary Howard, accused of murdering her four husbands. A few may know the true story of her lover, George Cutteford, a Plymouth 'cutty man' who became a Puritan lawyer. Cutteford was imprisoned in the horror of Lydford Gaol, persecuted by Mary's fourth husband, Sir Richard Grenville, the most notorious royalist General of the Civil War. But fewer still will know the secrets Cutteford died to protect – secrets that would destroy his own family; end Grenville's career; and make a boy with no name the richest landowner in Devon.

978 0 7524 6111 3

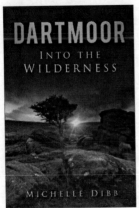

Dartmoor: Into the Wilderness
MICHELLE DIBB

Dartmoor is one of the few wilderness areas remaining in the UK – beautiful, mysterious and sometimes dangerous. From its rich, moss-covered ancient woodlands and rushing rivers to its sparse high moorland and bleak prison, Dartmoor has inspired artists, poets and musicians for centuries. This book contains a fascinating mixture of informative facts and mysterious tales. Here you will discover the wildlife, the history, the geography, the legends, the industry, the harshness and the inspiring wonder of one of England's most popular National Parks.

978 0 7524 5929 5

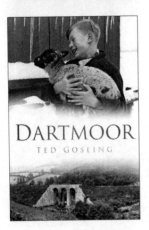

Dartmoor
TED GOSLING

Often called the last wilderness of southern Britain, Dartmoor combines wild open moorland, granite tors and wooded river valleys with areas of spectacular landscape. This collection presents a picture of life in and around Dartmoor from the end of the nineteenth century to the present day. It shows the people on Dartmoor, residents as well as tourists, and the characteristic industries in which they worked: tin mining, farming, quarrying and even the manufacture of gunpowder, many of which have disappeared to be replaced by an economy geared to tourism.

978 0 7509 2401 6

Visit our website and discover thousands of other History Press books.

www.thehistorypress.co.uk

Lightning Source UK Ltd.
Milton Keynes UK
UKOW05f0921240114

225189UK00001B/8/P